Rick am...
the kids and dog ahead of him

"Wow" was the truth. Despite his resistance, Kristin sat on the back of his mind 24/7. One look at her and he wanted to blast his saxophone until his music reached the heavens.

He took a breath. Slow down. Okay, so she intrigued him. So he admired her like no other woman he'd ever known. So he always looked forward to being with her. So what? It meant nothing. Or—it meant something.

Could this be love? Or at least the possibility of it? Or was it just his protective cop side making an appearance? He wasn't sure he knew the difference.

But more and more it seemed that getting himself straightened out might depend on having Kris in his life.

Dear Reader,

Morningstar Lake in the Catskill Mountains of New York State offers a refuge for people in need of healing. *Summer at the Lake* is about two people in search of that refuge: a city cop blaming himself for a hostage negotiation gone wrong and a mother trying to help her wounded daughter. Rick and Kristin try to remain aloof—each convinced the other is the last thing they need. But that's a losing proposition when Kristin's daughter, talented Ashley, falls in love with Rick's music and his dog. It's only a matter of time before the barriers come down.

I don't know why bad things happen to good people. And I'm horrified when bad things happen to children. What keeps me hopeful is seeing fear turn to courage when friends, neighbors and professionals provide unconditional support to those in need. I hope you'll be cheering at the end of the story, just as I did. My fingers couldn't type fast enough then!

I love hearing from readers. Please send me your comments about the story. You can reach me through my Web site, www.linda-barrett.com, or mail me at P.O. Box 841934, Houston, TX 77284-1934.

Happy reading!

Linda Barrett

SUMMER AT THE LAKE
Linda Barrett

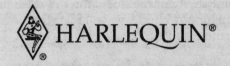

HARLEQUIN®

TORONTO • NEW YORK • LONDON
AMSTERDAM • PARIS • SYDNEY • HAMBURG
STOCKHOLM • ATHENS • TOKYO • MILAN • MADRID
PRAGUE • WARSAW • BUDAPEST • AUCKLAND

Recycling programs
for this product may
not exist in your area.

ISBN-13: 978-0-373-71560-2
ISBN-10:   0-373-71560-9

SUMMER AT THE LAKE

ABOUT THE AUTHOR

Linda has been writing for pleasure all her adult life, but targeted a professional career when she moved to Houston more than ten years ago. There she joined a local chapter of the Romance Writers of America and attended so many workshops and seminars, "I could have had a master's degree by now," she says. Five years later, in 2001, Harlequin Superromance published her debut novel, *Love, Money and Amanda Shaw*. When not writing, the mother of three grown sons ("all hero material like their dad") helps develop programs for a social service agency that works with the homeless.

Books by Linda Barrett

HARLEQUIN SUPERROMANCE

1115–THE INN AT OAK CREEK*
1192–THE HOUSE ON THE BEACH*
1218–NO ORDINARY SUMMER*
1256–RELUCTANT HOUSEMATES*
1289–THE DAUGHTER HE NEVER KNEW*
1366–A MAN OF HONOR
1409–HOUSEFUL OF STRANGERS

HARLEQUIN EVERLASTING LOVE

19–THE SOLDIER AND THE ROSE

*Pilgrim Cove

In honor of my friend,
Kate Lyons.

Intelligent, witty, loving
and courageous.

Acknowledgment

With many thanks to Kelle Z. Riley, author,
third-degree black belt and certified women's
self-defense instructor, for her enthusiasm and
the information she provided for this story.

Any errors are my own.

CHAPTER ONE

RICK COOPER SHOVED his badge and gun across his commanding officer's desk. "I'm done," he said quietly. "There will be no next time. Twelve years is enough." His mind made up, he eyeballed Captain Stein steadily.

The captain met his gaze with equal weight—and pushed the badge and weapon back at Rick. "Not accepted. Your resignation is not accepted."

"What?" Rick had imagined a dozen different conversations at this point, all variations on the theme of "Goodbye and good luck." He hadn't imagined this scene. "You can't…"

Stein held up his hand in a stop motion. "Save it. And you listen to me."

As if he had a choice.

"You're so lost in this incident that you can't see straight. Sure, it sucked. Sure, we hated the outcome. But I'm not losing my best negotiator to a pity party he's throwing for himself. And that's what you're doing."

Rick started to rise.

"Sit! I'm not finished."

He normally liked the captain. Stein was fair, smart and capable. But right now, Rick wanted to flatten him. Pity party! Didn't the man understand? Three people had died because of Rick's failure, one of them a little girl. Best negotiator? Hell, no.

"Did you talk to the shrink?" asked Stein. "No. Did you contribute to the debriefing with the team? No. Did you seek me out? No. I thought we had a better rapport than that."

"There's nothing to say," replied Rick. "The crisis team was there—every member. We played to win and we lost. Big-time. It won't happen again if I'm gone."

"Listen to your ego. Do you think you're the only one grieving this? The only person in the NYPD who's ever lost a negotiation?"

"Sorry, Captain. I'm done."

Stein shook his head. "It was a bad one, Rick. I know it. When a kid is involved, it's tough. But you're not done. You're burned out. And for that we have a leave of absence. Eight weeks."

Rick shrugged. It didn't matter what it was called— a leave, a resignation, whatever. He'd invested twelve years here for nothing, and now he was going to find another line of work, rethink the whole career angle. He wanted something less responsible, something that wouldn't be on his mind 24/7, something he was better suited for. Plus, with a less demanding job, he'd be ready for a social life again. A normal social life with a nice woman. A long-term relationship. Maybe a marriage that would last this time. The key was to leave the department first.

Again he started to get up.

"Uh, one more thing," said the captain.

"Yeah?"

Stein grunted. "I want to hear from you every week."

He had to be kidding. "I already have a mother."

The C.O. glared at him, his fist hitting the table as he said, "You're one of mine, Cooper, one of my best. And I take care of my own. Understand?"

He did. He understood the code, but Stein was going beyond the general brotherhood. The man had put the negotiating team together. His name was stamped on it, and Rick owed him more than a sarcastic response.

"I'll call you," Rick promised.

"And you'll call Doc Romano for an appointment."

"Romano? I don't need a shrink. I'm outta here, remember? In fact, I'm leaving town for a while. Going to do some fishing upstate, play my sax and find another career."

The C.O. continued to watch him. "Then you'll see the doc now. I did favors to get the guy assigned to us. He's the best there is, Cooper, and he's standing by for you."

Rick inhaled deeply, then exhaled. "Is that what you call taking care of your own?"

"That's exactly what I call it."

KRISTIN MCCARTHY SET the last of the dinner dishes into a cabinet in her borrowed house, delighted with the change of environment. She and Ashley would be country girls for a while. Her daughter needed distractions. New surroundings. Ashley needed a place to heal. Kristin's friend Marsha had immediately offered them her summer home on Morningstar Lake in the Catskill Mountains, three hours northwest of New York City. They could stay free of charge until August, when Marsha and her family would come up themselves. At that point Kristin would need to return to U.S. Life Corporation, anyway. Her leave of absence ran out on August 1.

She wondered how much progress her eleven-year-old would make by August, if any. Healing the soul seemed to take more time than healing the body.

She glanced at Ashley now as her daughter swept the floor and put the broom away. She watched her adjust each chair until it was positioned just so and then organize her schoolbooks for the next morning's work. In the week they'd been here, they'd established a few routines. Schoolwork began the day. Eating dessert on the screened porch overlooking the lake ended it.

The teakettle whistled. Kristin shut the heat off and glanced at Ashley. "Ready for a glass of milk and some of those peanut butter cookies we baked this afternoon?"

The child's wan smile broke her heart. Ash was a shadow of her naturally ebullient self, but Kristin continued the one-sided conversation as though nothing was wrong. If she kept acting as if life was normal, maybe Ashley would start to believe it could be normal again. Maybe she'd want to go back to school and play with her friends.

"Pour yourself some milk, sweetheart, and let's head out back to the porch. We can listen to the sounds of the lake."

First Ashley checked the locks on the front door, then she poured her milk. Half a glass. Kristin took comfort that it was whole milk. Four percent fat. Every calorie counted.

She snatched two sweaters from a wall hook, and collected the pencil and notebook the therapist had recommended they keep close by—in case Ashley had any breakthroughs to record. Then Kristin and Ash sat on matching chaises staring into the darkening night. The large lake began fifty feet from the house, and on sunny days, willows, birches and maple trees provided shade. There was a well-defined path to the water and shoreline, an area covered with small stones and sand.

She and Ashley had explored a lot of shoreline during the past few days. Whether they'd trespassed on neighboring properties, Kristin didn't know and didn't care. She considered the explorations around the lake "nature walks" and justified them as part of the science curriculum. Ashley seemed to enjoy examining the different plants and insects on these outings, so they'd made their walks a daily activity.

"The frogs make me laugh," said Kristin. "But the sounds of the water are soothing. What do you think?"

Ash nodded and imitated a gentle wave's rolling motion with her right arm, her fingers touching her left hand, repeating the sequence several times.

"That's right, Ash. The small waves lap the shore over and over," responded Kristin. "In a steady rhythm. Is that what you're telling me?"

Ashley nodded once more.

One day, her daughter would talk again. One day they'd chatter away about everything just like they used to. Even the psychologist said it would happen at some point. But Dr. Kaplan would make no predictions. "Every person works through it differently—there's no timetable for trauma recovery."

They'd get there, little by little. Kristin believed it. She *had* to believe it. Hope kept her going. Right now, however, maybe a game of Scrabble would keep

Ashley's mind occupied. The game might take an hour, but the longer the child stayed awake, the more tired she became and the less chance a nightmare would tear her apart. It worked for Kristin.

"Ash, how about…"

But Ashley jumped from her chaise, grabbed Kristin's hand and pointed to the left. The child cupped her own hand behind her ear.

Kristin listened hard and heard the lovely sounds of a… She glanced at Ashley. "A trumpet?"

Ash shook her head with vigor. Her chest rose and fell. Kristin heard deep breaths fill her daughter's lungs, heard her exhale, and stopped breathing herself. *Talk, baby, talk!*

"Ahh…ahhh…" The girl grabbed a pencil and wrote, "jazz sax."

Almost. She almost said it.

Ash positioned a chair to face the music and slowly sat down. As she listened, she remained perfectly still, hands in her lap.

In the glow of the overhead light, Kristin soon saw a tiny smile emerge on Ashley's face and wanted to shout for joy. The old Ashley—the real Ashley—was still there. Just now, the new Ashley had forgotten to be afraid, and had unconsciously allowed herself to enjoy the moment. The real Ashley was simply in hiding. Waiting. And the music had reached her.

It made sense. Ash was her father's daughter, too, a musical child of a talented dad who'd taught in high schools with passion and devotion—and played trumpet and piano with their regional orchestra.

John and a younger Ashley had filled the house with music at one time. Piano duets. Piano and flute duets.

Wonderful music. But John's unexpected death from a brain tumor four years ago... Kristin looked at Ashley again and caught her breath. Her daughter's quiet behavior, her fragility, were heartbreakingly similar to her demeanor then. *Grief.* She and Ashley had grieved hard together. And now her daughter, while listening to this sweet music, was mourning once again. For her dad? Or for herself?

Kristin's hands fisted. If she ever found the man who'd raped her child...she'd kill him. Piece by piece, she'd take him apart.

Right. She, who'd rarely engaged in a verbal argument, let alone a physical one, had absolutely no idea how to take a man down. It had been the cops' job to get the monster. And they hadn't done a blessed thing.

Ashley walked over and stroked her mother's tear-streaked face.

"The music's beautiful but sad," Kristin explained.

Her daughter nodded and bestowed a warm kiss on her cheek before sitting down again.

Kristin swallowed her sobs and allowed the anger to storm through her body all the way to her fingertips and toes, and to her cramped stomach. Oh, yes. She'd definitely kill the guy.

AFTER WARMING UP THE SAX the previous night, his first evening at his family's country house, Rick actually slept through until noon. Unbelievable. Maybe cutting out the caffeine was key, but he didn't think so. He gave credit to inhaling the sweet mountain air, removing himself from the "incident," and being in a place of good memories and happy times.

Over the years, his dad had turned a three-room cabin into a four-bedroom, fully winterized and insulated home. Rick had helped with the continuous remodeling, and for the last dozen years the family had enjoyed not only summers in the mountains, but ski weekends in the winter, too.

None of the neighbors were at the lake this early in the summer. Of course, that would change with the Memorial Day weekend at the end of the month. But for now, Rick had everything he wanted—his dog, his sax, some groceries and a change of environment.

The combination seemed to be working well so far.

On his second night, he headed for the screened back porch again, saxophone in hand, the big shepherd at his side. He suspected that Quincy enjoyed the companion-ship more than the music; the dog would stick close even if he played like a beginner, squealing and screech-ing sour notes. He wasn't a beginner. Music was the other half of himself.

Tomorrow, he'd call some of the local clubs and see if he could sit in on a few sets. That would be a treat he didn't often get in the city. The club owners knew him, knew he could hold his own with their players. Moreover, having an extra cop on the premises was always a plus. It was a fair trade. But now he wondered whether he could earn his living through music. Lots of people turned their hobbies into careers. Maybe he could be one of them.

The dog nuzzled him and waited until he sat down. Then Quincy lay on the braided area rug near his human's chair.

Rick fingered a few scales, closed his eyes and began

with some old favorites from John Coltrane. After ten minutes, he heard Quincy move, and through slitted lids saw him sit at attention, ears up, staring through the right-side screen. Rick didn't stop playing. His dog possessed superior hearing skills, and an owl, a frog, a cat or even a tiny field mouse could be out there. No big deal.

But then he heard the voice. A clear soprano. She began vocalizing against his melody—no words, just creating her own riffs. She kept up with him as he played. Out of curiosity, he changed musical styles, selecting a Sinatra standard, then something from Broadway. She stayed with him. He switched to the blues. To his astonishment, the lovely human vocals were replaced by the sound of a flute. And, like the vocals, this music followed his lead, too. Then led him. The flute wound around his sax, playing with the melody, playing against the melody. For almost an hour, he ran with the flow they created until, without conscious planning, he began Eric Clapton's "Tears in Heaven."

Boom! Red blood on a white jersey, the blood staining his memory as surely as it stained the child's clothing. An innocent little girl. A man. A woman. Arms and legs awry. Because of him. Tears welled, and this time, when the clear melody of the flute joined him, he heard the pure sound of a solitary church bell in his mind. The sax dropped to his lap. His head dropped to his hands. But the sweet, sad melody of the flute continued to the very end.

When quiet filled the air once more, he whispered a gravelly "Amen" and listened to the night. He heard only the gentle rustle of the leaves. Like an arthritic old man, Rick rose from his chair, reached for his sax and shuffled to the door.

His unknown partner was an accomplished musician, perhaps professional. Funny, he thought he knew everyone on this side of the lake. It seemed he was wrong.

FOR THE FIRST TIME since her daughter's rape, Kristin prepared for bed feeling content. Ash had reached out with music that night. She'd connected with someone. Kristin pulled down the bedspread and plumped the pillows, looking forward to a full night's sleep. A rare night's sleep.

Everything Ashley had done that evening, she'd done of her own volition. Her voice was an instrument and, unconsciously, Ash had joined the saxophone, singing without words. That activity alone had sent Kristin's spirits soaring, but when her daughter grabbed the flute—a last-minute addition to their luggage when leaving home—and played counterpoint to her mysterious partner, Kristin fought to keep her cheers to herself.

She slid into bed and reached for the notebook she kept in her night table drawer—a record of Ashley's progress. A journal of events. She hoped and prayed that whoever played the sax that evening was a youngster like Ash—a teenager would be fine. A sweet, gentle girl or boy who might help to draw her daughter out of the shell she'd created. Created because of a monster.

Kristin's palm stung. Glancing down, she saw her fisted hand, knuckles white and nails pressed hard against her skin. The purple indentations would last a long while. Every time she thought about what had happened to Ash… No, no. She had to forget the bastard. Focus on Ashley. Help her. Even if the monster was never caught, Ashley had to move forward and live her life. Maybe by August, her daughter would start acting like the energetic girl she'd been instead of the timid child she'd become. And if, God willing, she did, Kristin would never, ever complain about her messy bedroom again. She hated Ash's current need for perfection in every room. Another reminder of the monster.

She made notes about Ashley's participation in that night's concert, then turned out the lamp and sought a comfortable position. They were making some progress, and tomorrow might be even better than today. Maybe she should forcefully encourage Ashley to speak. The therapist said Ashley would talk when she was ready, but it was hard to straddle the line between gentle encouragement and overexpectation. Finally, Kristin told herself that she was doing the best she could and went to sleep.

Her hope for a better day crashed the next morning when she stood with Ashley on the front porch. Jogging down Lakeside Road—the blacktop route that circled the waterfront community—was a man and a dog. Sweat darkened the athlete's shirt, and the dog—well, the silver-black shepherd was gorgeous but humongous. And not leashed.

Ashley leaned against her.

"What's the matter, honey?"

Now, her child stepped behind her.

Kristin turned around. "Please, Ash. Talk to me. Tell me. Use words."

But Ashley pressed her lips together, her eyes wide and unblinking. Trancelike.

No, no, no. They didn't need any setbacks. She wouldn't force the issue, especially when she knew very well why Ashley was frightened. The man. The dog. Easy to see.

"Maybe they'll keep on running," Kristin said softly, "all the way out of sight. Maybe they live on the other side of the lake and that would be a couple of miles." And maybe pigs really did fly.

Her heart sank as, through the trees, she spotted the duo turn into a driveway two houses down—and sensed Ashley's retreat inside.

"Did you know, Ash," she said, intercepting her, "that the German shepherd is one of the most intelligent animals on the planet?" Whether this was actually a fact, she wasn't sure, but she didn't care. She took Ashley's hand and led her to the rocking chairs they'd set out upon their arrival the week before. "These dogs are so smart, they help the police detect hidden illegal drugs. They can find lost people just by sniffing a piece of their clothing before searching for them."

Ashley nodded, then opened her arms wide.

"Yes, the dogs are big. They have to be. They've got muscles for running and endurance for searching, and that helps them find a lost person."

Ashley rose and measured a four-foot height with her hand.

"Kids? Sure. They find kids as well as adults."

The girl's eyes brightened for a moment, then she shivered.

"What are you thinking, Ash?" *What threats had the monster made?* "Please, sweetheart. I can help you."

Ashley shook her head and stared at the floor. Kristin swallowed hard. Again, her daughter was shutting her out, refusing her help to ease the pain. To face the fear.

She leaned over and gave Ashley a kiss. "I love you, baby. Forever and ever. And nothing can change that."

The child hugged her tightly before glancing in the direction where the man and his companion had disappeared. Then she peered over her shoulder at their own front door.

But Kristin had had enough of hiding. No dog or man was going to prevent Ashley from feeling safe here, from enjoying herself outside, whether she was reading a book or swimming in the lake.

"Let's introduce ourselves, Ash. Then the dog will know we belong here, and we won't have to be concerned. If we bring some cookies, he'll love us forever. It's the neighborly thing to do. And if the dog can't eat them, the man will."

Kristin rose from the chair and motioned to her daughter. "Come on. We've got some peanut butter ones from yesterday's batch." She watched Ashley drag her feet into the house, but didn't change her mind about going to see their neighbors.

What should have taken a quick minute took ten with Ashley moving in slow motion. Finally, however, they stood in front of 68 Lakeside Road. Kristin knocked.

Thirty seconds later, the big man filled the doorway. He was fresh from a shower, with a towel around his neck, and wearing a water-spotted T-shirt and a different pair of running shorts. He studied them in silence for a moment, the dog sitting at perfect attention at his side. Kristin's heart sank. She hadn't counted on unfriendly neighbors.

And then he smiled, his steel-gray eyes melting to a soft gray mist. "Are you guys lost? I don't recognize you."

Whew! What a change. The hunk was friendly. Shocked at her thoughts, Kristin stood tongue-tied. She hadn't noticed any man in four years.

She handed the cookies to him and offered their names. "We're staying at the Goldman place until August. We saw you running with your...uh, pal here...your rather large pal...so we came to meet him. And you, too, of course." Her face burned. Her skin had to be cherry-red, the downside of being a fair-skinned blonde. To compensate, she thrust her chin up and forced herself to look directly at him.

"House-sitting for the Goldmans?"

"Something like that," she replied, this time smoothly. "Marsha is a good friend of mine."

He nodded and studied her as though memorizing her features for future reference. Then he turned toward Ashley and a pain-filled expression crossed his face.

Ashley's fingers touched Kristin's.

Immediately, the man smiled as if nothing had happened. "Rick Cooper," he said, extending his hand first to her, then to Ashley. "I'm happy to meet you both."

Kristin watched Ash's reaction. Slowly, without speaking, her daughter placed her hand in Rick's and let it remain for a complete handshake. Kristin exhaled in relief, knowing she'd record the action in the journal. It was important enough.

Now, he motioned them inside. A big country kitchen ran from front to back on the right side of the house. Oak floors, a large oak dining table. He took the cookies and led them to a breakfast nook in the back toward the lake. On the way, Kristin saw an informal library and game room on the left, a staircase and another room beyond it. Once in the breakfast nook, she noticed the large back porch and guessed that every house had a screened arrangement overlooking the lake. This was a house for a family.

"Do you have any kids?" she asked conversationally. "Ashley is eleven."

"I'm single. But my niece and nephew will be up at the end of the month."

Single by choice, she thought. His choice. With his looks and physique, he could attract a swarm. "We'll look forward to meeting them, too."

"If you ladies take a seat, I'll put Quincy through his paces and then introduce you up close and personal."

"Thank you, Rick. We really appreciate your time."

Rick gestured, and the dog sat at attention, watching his owner. With hand signals only, he had the dog sit, lie down, walk at heel, stay, ignore treats he'd placed on the floor, and shake hands with him. Perfect performance. The reward came quickly in the form of praise and one of the doggie treats. And applause from Kristin.

She didn't wait for Rick's invitation, but impulsively knelt down to pet the beautiful animal, scratching his head and crooning softly to him. She got a lick for her efforts. The beast was friendly and liked to nuzzle. She beamed at Ashley, totally reassured.

"Your turn, honey. He may be big, he may even resemble a gray wolf, but he's a lovable baby."

Ashley stayed seated.

Rick knelt next to the dog, held his collar and spoke softly to Ashley. "Where I live in the city, all the kids play with Quincy, and that's when he's the happiest. They throw balls for him, they roll on the ground with him, but most of all they hug him and talk to him." He winked at her, and said, "He's their special friend."

Ashley barely blinked.

"Right now," continued Rick, "Quincy's a little lonely." He spoke to the dog. "Are you sad, boy?"

The dog whined and licked him. "See what I mean, Ashley? Now it's Quincy who could use a special friend, a friend right here at Morningstar Lake."

He motioned to the child and smiled with such encouragement that Kristin held her breath, waiting for her daughter's response.

Without a word, Ashley slid from her chair and, step by cautious step, approached Rick from the side, avoiding a face-to-face with Quincy.

"See how fast he's wagging his tail? He's smiling at you, Ashley. Notice the way his tongue's hanging out of the side of his mouth? Man, I hate to admit this handsome boy looks silly, but he sure does."

Was that a giggle? Or a squeaky shoe? Kristin stared at Ashley, but her daughter was totally focused on Quincy. Could this be a turning point for her?

Continuing his soft patter, the man somehow maneuvered them to the front porch, the dog at heel next to Ashley, while she held his leash. The two walked up and down the entire width of the porch several times until Rick motioned them to stop. Quincy, however, didn't seem ready to lose his new friend. He tucked his head under Ashley's arm, looked up with adoring eyes and licked her cheek and neck. His tail wagged so hard its breeze gave Kristin goose bumps.

"He likes me!" The delight in Ashley's voice was unmistakable as she hugged the big canine.

Words! A sentence. Voluntarily uttered. Kristin couldn't move. Nor could she stop her tears—or the horrified expression on Rick's face when he saw them.

His reaction didn't matter. Her tears didn't matter. Only Ashley mattered. Ashley and her breakthrough. An entire sentence! Kristin would call Dr. Kaplan. Now they'd move forward. She just knew it.

CHAPTER TWO

THE LITTLE GIRL WAS a sweetheart, and her mom a real looker. Smart, too. Smart enough to visit him and Quincy. But something about his two neighbors didn't add up. Lots of kids had to get used to the dog—he was oversize, after all. But what was the woman crying about? The kid had finally relaxed and jumped into the conversation…and the mother cried? It made no sense.

Oh, hell. If life always made sense, Rick's fourteen hours of negotiation would have turned out differently, and three people would be alive right now. He figured Kristin and Ashley had their secrets and were entitled to them.

Thirty minutes after his neighbors left, he whistled for the hound, locked the house and got into his Honda Pilot. Quincy rode in the front passenger seat as usual, with a safety harness around him—air bag disengaged, of course. Traveling on what could be Main Street, USA, Rick made his way to the sheriff's office on the far side of town.

Ignoring Sam Keaton was not an option. The older man already knew Rick was at the lake. Not that Rick had spoken to him. He simply knew how Sam worked and how the town worked—news traveled, especially to the sheriff. Yesterday, Rick had purchased groceries and said hello to a few old friends, so someone was sure to have spread the word. Sam would be expecting him.

In the strip mall lot, he parked in a designated visitor's space and walked into the storefront office. It was a big room divided into functional areas, with Sam Keaton in the center of everything. The man had a private office as well, but in the ordinary course of events, he preferred to be in view if he wasn't on the road.

Sam greeted him with pleasure and a slap on the back, but with no surprise. Rick returned the greeting with a grin. "I see the party line's still working, huh?"

"You bet. Best system in the world," the officer replied as he leaned over to talk to Quincy while scratching the underside of his muzzle. The dog whined in pleasure while Rick helped himself to a cup of coffee.

"So, what brings you to Morningstar Lake?" asked Sam. "That's the part I don't know yet."

Before Rick could respond, however, Sam snapped his fingers. "Hey—were you called in to negotiate the hostage situation down the road in Oakridge the night before last? It came across the wires. A domestic thing. A man, wife and his two kids. Right up your alley. Just the sort of situation you handle all the time."

Rick's stomach knotted and nausea rose, but he put on his cop face, showing nothing. "Nope. I don't work those cases anymore, Sam. In fact, I'm not working any cases. I'm done." An inner calm descended as he said the words. "I'm here with Quincy, my saxophone and my fishing rod. In fact, we're heading toward Sweet Trout River right now."

Sam's gaze appeared to include X-ray vision, and Rick wasn't surprised to hear the sheriff say, "Well, I see you're still carrying your piece. But I like your plan. It's sound for a person who needs a break."

Rick put his foot up on a chair and leaned forward. "I'm not on a break, Sam. I'm open to ideas for a new direction."

"New direction, eh? Such as?" The man gave him his full attention.

"Such as…" Good question. His mind had been rolling with general ideas, but now he needed specifics. "How about hotel security? We've got a couple of those in the area. Or corporate security? Heck, parking lot security looks good to me now. I need something requiring less adrenaline than what I've done."

"Hmm. You want me to ask around?"

"Sure. I can relocate. I've got no family ties in the city to hold me back."

"Well," said the sheriff, "in this case, that's a good thing. But a security guard earns a fraction of what you earn now."

"Doesn't matter. I'd appreciate your help." His needs were small. He just had to become someone else.

"You've got it. Maybe I'll come up with something."

Something before next week would be good—before his first phone appointment with Doc Romano.

Rick cleared his throat. "Sam," he began, hating himself for asking, "how did the crisis in Oakridge work out?"

The sheriff's broad grin sent a wave of relief through Rick. "Good," Rick said. "I'm glad they had the right personnel." Someone competent had handled that situation.

"The towns share crisis teams," said Sam, "but sometimes we have to ask for outside help. I heard the negotiator came from downstate, and when you showed up…" He left the rest unsaid.

The sheriff crouched on the floor again and spoke to Quincy. "You've got a job to do, big boy. You've got to take care of this guy. And, while you're at it, you can watch out for those two little ladies nearby. The woman's on her own, and Marsha Goldman told me they could use a friend or two."

Friend? Well, Rick could volunteer for that job. No salary needed. Improving his social life was on his agenda, too. He eyed the dog. Even Quincy would be an asset. He was a sucker for kids.

HE LIKES ME!

Ashley's words had haunted Kristin for the rest of the day, into the night and into the following morning, as well. Her wonderful daughter was grateful for a dog's affection. It was beyond pathetic. It was pitiful. And Ash hadn't spoken again since she'd uttered those three words.

Disappointed and discouraged, Kristin was a sad case, too. Behind the wheel of her car the next afternoon, she felt like howling.

Prior to the rape, Ashley had been a people magnet. She'd been an outgoing child who made friends easily and naturally, with a half-dozen girlfriends who regularly came to the house. And as for the phone—had it been just a short while ago that Kristin had threatened to block all incoming numbers on Ashley's cell except the ones from Kris's office and their house? And now…

She turned toward Ashley, who was sitting in the passenger seat. "Seat belt buckled?"

The blond head moved up and down quickly.

"Come on, honey. You can talk now."

No response.

Obviously, her child had the skill. She'd spoken with the dog just yesterday.

"Should we kidnap Quincy?"

"Mom!" Ashley's horrified tone made Kristin laugh. *Gotcha, sweetheart.*

The dog was the key. Maybe Ashley felt safer with the big mutt. Maybe she thought general conversation with Kristin would lead to talking about the incident, so she said nothing. Maybe she was afraid her mother would ask a lot of questions again. Maybe this, maybe that. A lot of maybes when Kristin wanted answers.

Despite her disappointment, she tried not to push Ashley. She was careful to follow the advice of the therapist, who was using a bunch of manipulative materials—dolls, clay, art supplies, children's blocks—to encourage Ashley. But sometimes Kristin found it almost impossible to keep silent.

Her daughter had been visiting the psychologist every week since the rape, and Kristin hadn't seen much progress. She wanted her old Ashley back!

Moreover, if her daughter didn't improve, the police would never get a description of the attacker. The police. Another disappointment. It seemed to her they expected *Ashley* to solve the crime! What had they been doing in the interim? Sure, they'd assigned her an advocate, but that person had no new information. Just that the case was open and being investigated. How? Kristin didn't know. It all seemed to come back to Ash providing a description. But all the art supplies in the world were worth nothing if Ash didn't use them. The longer it took, the colder the case became. And Kristin wanted the bastard found. It had already been over seven weeks.

Twenty minutes later, she pulled into the parking lot of the regional library in Morningstar Lake, so she and Ash could do some research on dogs. Ashley had written a four-word note that morning: "Library—Dogs—German shepherds." Obviously, she wanted to learn about the breed, and Kristin thought it was a great idea. Any idea that excited Ashley was fine with her. Their neighbor's dog had certainly earned her approval for the magic he'd performed. *He likes me!* Pathetic or not, Kristin was grateful for the three-word sentence.

AT 1:30 P.M., Ashley was the only school-age child in the library. Kristin noticed that immediately. And of course, it made sense, but… But what? What was she hoping for? That a lovely age-mate would suddenly appear, a contemporary of Ashley's, another good student who loved to read like her daughter did? A girl who could be a friend? *Damn it, Kristin. Live in reality.* Ash wouldn't talk to her own friends at home, so why would she talk to a stranger?

"Come on, honey. Let's go find the reference section on dogs."

Normalcy. That's what she'd been hoping for.

Ashley pointed to a sign on the main desk that read Library Cards Here.

It appeared her daughter expected to return home with a bunch of books. "Let's ask."

The librarian's name was Anne Rules, according to another sign. Ashley grinned when she pointed it out to Kristin. "Funny, huh?" Kristin whispered.

"I think it is," said the woman behind the desk. One with excellent hearing. "We do have rules in the library, but we're a friendly place, too. How may I help you ladies?" When she smiled, her eyes crinkled in the corners and a dimple appeared at the side of her mouth. Clearly, she loved her job.

Kristin introduced Ashley and herself. "We'll be at the lake for a couple of months, so we'll need library cards."

Anne Rules reached for some forms and flyers, then turned her attention to Ashley. "We have some wonderful activities for young people. Look at this." She pointed to a neon-green flyer.

"Next week, we have a poetry slam—always lots of fun. We have an American Girl Book Club going on right now. And when school ends, we'll start our Summer Festival of Books. You're right on time to join in."

Hope bloomed in Kristin again. Perfect timing! Ashley was so creative not only with music, but also with writing. These activities should draw her in.

The librarian was handing Ash a flyer. "Here, Ashley, take it with you as a reminder. And oh, I almost forgot. We serve doughnuts and apple cider to everyone who comes." Ms. Rules beamed at the child as if she were offering her the world tied up in a pretty bow.

Kristin eagerly turned to her daughter. "What do you think…" And knew it would never happen.

Ashley stood frozen, staring at the poster.

"Maybe in a week or two, honey, when we've been here longer?" She was grasping at straws. She knew it and couldn't help it.

Then Ms. Rules leaned across the desk and spoke directly to the child. "Your mom can come, too, Ashley.

I know it's hard to be the new girl and not know anybody. I'm sure you'll make some friends very soon."

From her mouth to God's ears. Kristin held her hand out to Anne. "Thank you. No wonder Marsha loves her summers here. If everyone is as friendly as you, who wouldn't be happy?" She glanced at her daughter again. "We'll try to come soon. Won't we, Ash?"

Ashley remained silent. However, she picked up a pencil from the desk and wrote on the pretty flyer: "Dogs. German shepherds." She handed the note to Anne.

Kristin sighed. Her daughter managed to communicate all right, in her own way, to get what she wanted.

They searched the shelves and found a treasure trove of dog books. Ash's eyes sparkled at one in particular, which pictured a German shepherd on the cover, a dog with Quincy's coloring. She placed that one on top of her pile and sat at an empty table near the stacks while Kristin browsed for some fiction.

She hadn't read many novels lately. Her reading time had been spent delving into books on post-traumatic stress disorder, child abuse and the nature of recovery— not topics she'd have chosen ordinarily. After making her selections, she walked toward Ashley, who was nose deep in a book. Taking an extra moment to study her child, Kristin saw the Ashley she'd seen hundreds of times in the past. In this library, at this moment, she saw what she'd been praying to see—a glimpse of normalcy. Ashley involved in a familiar activity. Reading. Satisfying her curiosity. Ashley being Ashley.

Kristin bit her lip. Why, oh why had she taken the girls to the movies that day? And why hadn't she taught Ashley never to go to the restroom by herself? If only she had, Ash wouldn't have been so vulnerable. She probably would have escaped. If only Kristin had been a better mother.

LIGHTNING FLASHED in the distance. Thunder rumbled. Fat raindrops plopped, then picked up speed. Rick reeled in his line, annoyed at having been caught unaware. The price he paid for daydreaming. Well, not exactly daydreaming, he amended. Just emptying his mind of the past. Filling it with the present—fishing, hiking, great music, his new neighbors. And the future—a new, no-stress career.

The storm was in his immediate future, however, and he quickly packed up his rod and tackle box and headed to his vehicle. As soon as Quincy saw him, he crawled out from beneath the car.

Fifteen minutes later, Rick headed slowly back through town, his stomach now rumbling along with the thunder. Eventually, he pulled into the parking lot of Dora's Diner on Main Street. Great Cooking, Big Portions—What More Can U Want? Her red neon slogan flashed on the roof, the bright letters standing out like a beacon while he drove through the torrents.

His wasn't the only car in the lot, so the beacon seemed to be working. A mix of delicious aromas hit him as soon as he opened the door. Dora hadn't lost her touch.

"Ricky Cooper! The dog, too? Well, come on in. Quincy's always welcome here—he's a working dog, isn't he? So take any seat you want, but act fast, we're filling up."

Ricky. Only Dora still called him that. "Thanks, Dora. I don't care what you cook, just make a lot."

The woman hoo-ha'd, as he knew she would, and waved him away. He immediately headed for the corner booth against the front wall opposite the counter, his usual preference. From here, he could see the complete interior as well as the street outside. He waved or nodded at a number of people as he walked, automatically taking mental notes.

By the time he sat down, his server was bringing him an ice-cold beer and promising dinner in a matter of minutes.

"The brew's on the house," she said, nodding at the drink.

"Thanks, but add it to the bill."

"No can do. She's the boss." The waitress nodded toward Dora, then disappeared. Sometimes it was easier to go along, but he'd rather pay his own way.

He stretched his legs behind the hound and took his first swallow of the draft. It slid down well. He leaned back, relaxed in this familiar environment. Comfortable. No adrenaline rush. A good thing. A very good thing.

The door opened again, and the stormy day got brighter. Two familiar rain-soaked blondes stood in the entrance, looking lost and hopeful.

The hostess shook her head and pointed toward the counter seats at the end of the row. There were no booths left. His neighbors started walking his way, and the girl—Ashley—spotted him first. He wasn't fooled by her delighted expression. It wasn't because of him. He winked at her and motioned toward the floor, under the table.

She quickly poked her mom's arm, pointed at Rick and trotted over. Without a word to him, she just crouched down and hugged Quincy, who promptly kissed her and whined with affection.

"I'm so sorry," began Kristin when she reached him.

As he automatically stood up, he took a moment to study her expression. "No, you're not. You're actually damn glad. And that's fine."

The woman glanced first at him, then at her daughter, whose thin arms were wrapped around Quincy's neck, her head resting on his shoulders with a sweet and contented smile.

"You're absolutely right," she admitted. "I'm not merely 'damn glad,' I'm overjoyed. I know you don't understand—"

He interrupted. "Would you like to sit down and join me instead of using the counter? I highly recommend the pot roast."

Her smile warmed him better than the beer. "Thanks. I think we will. And pot roast sounds great. We both like it. But Ash…" She bent down toward her daughter. "When our food arrives, you sit up here with us."

Rick signaled the waitress to take their orders and bring them with his.

When Kristin straightened up again, her eyes were suspiciously shiny. She leaned toward him. "Ash said, 'Okay.'"

She'd been correct earlier. He didn't understand everything yet, so he said nothing, just waited. He'd been good at patience in his old job.

Not so Kristin, it seemed. She put her hand on his bare arm, her touch hot on his skin. Her smile was so enchanting, so eager, he could only stare.

"My daughter is talking to him—again!"

"And?"

She blinked hard, but couldn't prevent tears. And suddenly he felt himself being pulled under to a place he didn't want to be. He was ready for a social life—a summer romance, a fling. Sam had told him Kristin didn't have a husband, so he wasn't crossing any lines there. But Rick certainly had no plans to take on a woman with serious problems.

Kristin blotted her cheek, and smiled at him. "This might be a breakthrough for her, so thank you. Thank you for having Quincy at the right place at the right time for Ashley. I cannot believe that a dog—a dog!—got her to speak again."

Oh, yeah. Serious problems. "He's pretty special," Rick replied quietly.

She regained her composure. "I'll say he's special. Ash and I will never forget him. In fact, she took out several books about German shepherds from the library today. Maybe I can incorporate her enthusiasm into the curriculum I'm using—maybe with some essays."

"Curriculum? She's not in school?"

"I've been homeschooling her recently. It's—it's better that way, for now."

His eyes narrowed in speculation, but she offered nothing more. This mother hen was protecting her chick. Or thought she was.

Their dinners arrived then. Heaving a big sigh, Ashley stood up, ready to slide in next to her mother. "You need to wash your hands," Kristin said. "They were all over the dog."

Her daughter didn't move.

"I'll go with you." She excused herself, and the two departed.

Every instinct of Rick's, every nerve ending, thrummed with suspicion. He'd had too much experience with victims not to recognize the signs. Damn, damn, damn. That fragile little girl… He didn't need this.

The ladies returned and they all dug into their dinners. Even Ashley.

"I guess Dora knows how to make a good pot roast, huh, Ashley?" Rick asked.

The girl nodded and placed a slice on her napkin. She pointed down.

There were big rules and small rules. In the great scheme of things, he'd be breaking a small one. It was a no-brainer to give the child a big moment, for the sake of making her happy. "Normally, I don't feed Quincy from the table. It's not good manners for a dog. But since today seems pretty special, go for it."

The kid beamed at him and ducked beneath the table.

Rick chuckled and looked at Kristin. "If you really want her to write an essay about Quincy, just ask. He has an interesting history."

Quincy was the safest topic he could think of. He wasn't about to ask any personal questions about Ashley or Kristin. He needed his zone of safety. Quincy was it.

"Okay," said Kristin. "I'm asking. Tell me about your dog."

"To start with, I didn't buy Quincy. I saw him online and applied for him through a rescue organization."

Kristin angled her head to see Quincy better. "You've got to be kidding me. He's absolutely gorgeous and simply perfect."

Ashley popped back up and started eating again.

"Guess what, honey?" Kristin asked. "Mr. Cooper saved Quincy's life and gave him a great home. He rescued him. Isn't that amazing?"

Rick didn't want the kid to look at him as though he were Santa Claus. But she did. He didn't want her to think he sprinkled stars in the night sky. But her eyes were rounder than dinner plates and shinier than a big harvest moon. A piece of his heart started to rip.

"Many people do what I did," he said quickly. "It's nothing special."

Ashley nodded her head up and down so fast he thought it would snap. She made a writing motion.

Kristin covered her hand. "No, Ash. *Tell* us. Or tell Quincy."

The kid inhaled and exhaled, looked ready to cry, and Rick braced himself. Then she took a single huge breath. "It is a big deal," she said, the words tumbling over themselves. "You *saved* him!"

And no one had saved her.

The cry in her voice slammed into his gut. His heart. He knew it would echo in his memory for the rest of his life.

A HUGE LIGHTNING BOLT cracked close by and a second one followed, illuminating the street outside their large window, a street still being pelted with heavy rain. Most cars crawled by, their drivers hunched over the wheels. Others passed more quickly, showering the sidewalks with water.

Rick shook his head in disgust. Those drivers couldn't see an inch in front of their noses. They needed to slow down. Suddenly, the electric lights inside the diner blinked on and off, then went out. Ashley moaned and leaned against her mother. A low murmur buzzed through the place.

Rick heard Kristin shush her daughter, tell her not to worry. They were safe in the diner. And they were together.

He was about to concur, when—*crash!* Metal on metal. The sound outside made him flinch, made him clench his teeth. Another smash. And a third. At least two cars. He wouldn't know how bad it was until he got outside.

He stood up and quickly said to his companions, "You guys stay here. Please don't attempt to drive back yet, Kristin." Then he looked at the dog. "Quincy, take care of the girls." He motioned with his hand, and the big dog took his position in front of the booth, sitting at attention.

Jogging to the door, he called over his shoulder to Dora, "Get 911. Call Sam's office. Do you have any lanterns? Emergency lights. Flashlights. Blankets. Anything." He peered through the restaurant. "I need a couple of people to direct traffic. Get the flashlights first."

He didn't wait to see who responded, trusting many would. Outside, two cars sprawled across Main Street, each one heavily dented front and side. No one was outside either vehicle.

Damn. Head-on. Spinning. There would be injuries. He approached the first car and pulled the door open. Two youngsters—teenagers by his judgment—lay in the front seat. He checked airways, breathing, constrictions. They were unconscious, but breathing. He wanted to get some blankets on them to keep them warm and prevent shock.

Other people joined him. "Block off the street with

your cars. Use your headlights and flashers. Ambu-
lances only."

He approached the second car and heard a baby
crying. *Good.* Lungs functioned. He pulled at the
driver's bashed-in door, but couldn't budge it. He could
see a young woman, not moving, her head to one side,
her air bag half-inflated. He ran to the passenger door,
managed to pry it open, and knelt on the front seat. Was
the driver breathing? He put his hand on her chest. Felt
a shallow rise and fall.

Yes!

"You're going to be fine. If you can hear me, just
know that. You'll be fine. Your baby is fine. Making a
lot of noise. We'll take care of your infant."

He backed out of the car, looking for assistance, and
found it. People had blankets, and a neighbor recognized the car and went in the back with the baby.

The rain let up. He heard the wail of sirens and, in the
near distance, spotted the first ambulance. Ten minutes
later, the second ambulance was loaded and on its way
to the E.R. Rick was in the midst of reports, working
with the sheriff's department and county deputies. He'd
been the first "officer" on the scene, and even though he
wasn't in uniform, he continued the paperwork.

Finally, he made his way back inside the diner. People
slapped him on the shoulder, and compliments and words
of appreciation flew his way. He hid behind the situation.

"There's more, folks. Listen up. There's no electricity for a hundred miles, and there's flash flooding on
the Thompsonville Road, Lookout Point and Grove
Highway leading to the state road. You know, all the
usual spots. Avoid them when you drive home. Thanks."

He headed toward his table. He wanted tea. Coffee. Something burning hot.

Just then, Kristin smiled at him, and he started to sweat. That drowning feeling was coming over him again, and it had nothing at all to do with the storm outside.

He slid into the booth and focused on Ashley. "Was Quincy a good boy?" he asked.

"Oh, yes. I think he's my friend."

"Without a doubt, Ashley. He's definitely your friend."

Kristin was silent, her glance moving from Ashley to him. Just listening, a tiny smile making a constant appearance. He wondered how long it had been since she'd heard Ashley participate in a conversation. Maybe to her it was like hearing music.

"Mr. Cooper?"

"Yes, Ashley?"

"You know what else? I think you're everybody's friend. You helped everybody today. Didn't he, Mom?"

"He sure did."

Maybe the floor could open up and swallow him. "I'm going to get something hot to drink. Dora has gas stoves. They're probably working."

"You can run, but you can't hide."

Kristin was laughing at him. And man, she was beautiful.

"Hot chocolate?" asked Ashley.

"You got it, sweetheart. Anything you want."

KRISTIN WATCHED the big man retreat to the front of the restaurant. He'd taken charge of the situation as though he'd been handling emergencies all his life. Was that what was known as a born leader? Or…or… Oh, God. Her next thought was not acceptable. Nah, he couldn't be a cop. That just wouldn't be fair. She wanted to like the guy.

"I like Mr. Cooper," said Ashley very slowly, as if she read her mother's mind. "Even though he's bossy."

Immediately, Kristin assessed her daughter's expression. Bossy was not a positive description.

"I suppose you could say he's bossy," she repeated calmly, waiting for more.

"But in a good way," said Ash. "He helped everybody. He told us all what to do."

Her heart started to race. Her daughter was really talking now, and Kristin gave full credit to the dog. Quincy had been key. The shepherd continued to sit right next to a relaxed Ashley at their dark and cozy table. Perhaps Kristin was about to have her first meaningful conversation with her child since the attack.

"Tell me a little more," Kristin encouraged.

Ashley patted her hand. "Mr. Cooper's taking care of us, Mom. And that's very good."

Her newly brightened world dimmed again.

CHAPTER THREE

MR. COOPER'S TAKING CARE of us, Mom. Her daughter's last words at the diner were not what she had expected to hear. Or wanted to hear. In the early hours of the morning following her unplanned visit to Dora's Diner, after driving behind Rick's vehicle at a snail's pace when the rain had eased up, Kristin should have been sound asleep. Instead, she tossed and turned.

She punched her pillow a dozen times. *She* was the one Ashley needed to trust. *She* was the mother. The adult. The one who'd given birth to her, and the one person on earth who loved her the most. Ashley knew that. Her daughter knew she was loved. But obviously, her child had needs Kristin wasn't meeting. And she didn't have to be a shrink to figure it out. Ashley thought Kristin had let her down, and now she couldn't trust her mother to keep them safe. Kristin had dropped her daughter off at the movies—at the mall—and a horrible thing had happened. Of course, Ashley and Sabrina had enjoyed Saturday matinees many times before that particular day. Kristin or Jo Anne had always been on time to pick their girls up afterward. They'd trained their daughters to call them on their cells immediately at the end of the film.

None of those reassurances mattered on that one horrible day Ashley would remember for the rest of her life. On that horrible day when Kristin hadn't been there to protect her. And that was the bottom line for Ashley. The poor kid probably wanted—would prefer—her adoring dad. Kristin had certainly yearned for John's help in getting Ash through this experience, wondering what advice he'd have given, what he'd have done differently.

But she didn't have John anymore. In fact, she barely had family support. She'd been doing the best she could on her own, hoping it was enough. Now, she had doubts. She had to continue to be strong, however, for everyone's sake.

Her parents were wonderful—she loved them dearly—but they could hardly bring themselves to believe what had happened to their only grandchild. In their midseventies, they'd hovered like a pair of dainty hummingbirds, treating Ash like breakable porcelain. In the beginning, when Kristin and Ash had stayed with them before coming to Morningstar Lake, maybe that had been okay. But it wasn't anymore. John's parents, so loyal and loving, called regularly but had retired to Florida. When they'd visited immediately after the event, they hadn't been any calmer than Kristin's parents. In the end, Kristin had somehow managed to reassure them that all would be well.

But would it? Ashley recognized Rick Cooper as someone she could trust—a strong, confident personality. She also trusted the dog. She didn't trust her own mother.

Kristin flinched as that thought took shape, but she simply didn't know what more to do except to live each day and be Ashley's cheerleader. Thank goodness she'd gotten an extended leave of absence from work. Unpaid, so she'd had to sharpen her money-stretching skills, but at least her job was secure. U.S. Life Corporation wasn't the worst company to work for, she reflected. She rolled over again, breathing deeply and evenly, trying to find silver linings and a way to fall asleep. Finally, she drifted off.

Brilliant sunlight flooded her room the next morning and woke her. Brilliant sunlight and a knock at her bedroom door. She glanced at her battery-powered clock radio. Eleven! She couldn't remember the last time she'd slept that late.

"Come on in, Ash."

Her daughter entered and the aroma of freshly brewed coffee teased Kristin. Ash held out a mug.

"You made coffee?"

Ash shook her head. "Rick."

"Rick? What happened to calling him Mr. Cooper? And is he here?"

Again a shake.

Kristin sank back against her pillows. "That's a relief. I'm not even coherent yet."

Ashley pointed toward the front of the house. "He's on our porch."

Kristin reached for the mug, delighted by the possibility of a conversation with Ashley. "He'll have to wait. I need this." She took a sip. "Mmm…it's good."

Ash didn't reply, so Kristin kept the dialogue going alone. "Isn't it awesome how clear and beautiful the day is, after yesterday's storm?"

Ashley went to the light switch and moved it up and down. "There's no electricity yet."

Kristin briefly wondered how Rick had made the coffee, but before she could voice her thought, Ash waved quickly and left the room. End of conversation. But if the dog was outside, then Kristin couldn't compete.

She shrugged and finished the drink before washing up. A shower would come later, when hot water returned. She dressed in jeans and a white jersey, then added a pair of socks and running shoes to complete her uniform for country living. She pulled her hair back into a low ponytail, brushed her bangs and was set.

When she stepped outside with her empty mug, Ashley was with the dog in the yard, practicing commands, and Rick was sitting on the top step, untangling fishing line. He leaned against the wooden railing, head bent over his work, a lock of dark hair falling on his forehead. He hummed softly as he concentrated, but she didn't recognize the tune.

He said good-morning without turning his head a fraction.

"Do you hear as well as Quincy does?" she joked, sitting on the opposite side of the step, leaning against the support post. Without waiting for a reply, she added, "Thanks for the coffee, neighbor. It hit the spot."

"You're welcome." He held out a length of line, examined the knots and grunted, then resumed his work.

He was about as conversational as her daughter. "So, how'd you manage to brew it without electricity?" Exciting subject.

"Our gas grill has a burner on the side. Used my mom's old aluminum coffeepot."

"No wonder it tasted so delicious."

"Is it a big enough bribe for you to help me with these

tiny knots?" He opened his hands and shook his head. "Your fingers have got to be smaller than mine."

"Bring it on," she said, glad to help out a man who'd helped so many others last night. *Last night...*

He handed her the filament and sat one step below her, resting his elbows on the porch floor, gazing at the sturdy maple and oak trees lining the road.

"About last night..." she began as she tackled the fishing line.

"Sounds like the title of a movie," he joked. But when she glanced at him, he turned away.

Her intuition started humming. The guy wasn't as confident and carefree as he tried to appear. She'd try a different approach.

"So, Rick, are you taking an early vacation? It's only the middle of May."

"You could say that and be right."

"Oh, come on. Don't be coy. You can't be any older than I am—much too young for early retirement!"

He chuckled. "You caught me. Not retired. I just resigned. Or, as the department put it, took a leave of absence."

Her stomach dropped. She pursued anyway. "The department?" She glanced at Ashley, who was playing with the dog, then focused back on Rick.

This time, he studied her before responding. "The NYPD. Twelve years."

"Damn it! I thought so. No wonder you handled the emergency so well last night. No wonder Ashley feels so safe with you." *Of all the gin joints...*

"And that makes you upset?" Frown lines creased his forehead.

"Yes. No. Yes. Somewhat." Seemed he wasn't the only confused person in the conversation. She yanked the line and he winced.

"Oops. Maybe I should take that fishing line back."

She couldn't blame him. Her hands were shaking. She dropped them in her lap. "Give me a sec. I just have to get used to the idea that I've got a cop living two doors down."

Rick had to set her straight. "Ex-cop. Remember that."

"Does it really matter?" she retorted. "I swear, Quincy has more brains, has had more success and cares more about Ashley than the entire Mayfield police force."

Rick stood up. It was time to get out of Dodge. A new career did not include backsliding into his old one. "I can leave the dog with her if you like. Just tell him to go home when you're ready."

He reached for the ball of filament.

She held on to it. "I'm sorry. I shouldn't have painted you with the same brush I used on my incompetent hometown department on Long Island."

She was so wrong. "Go right ahead, Kris. You're entitled. I've made my share of mistakes, too. I'd like to be perfect. Hell, we all would. But…we're also human. More's the pity." He mumbled the last words to himself, but she probably heard them.

"Then it's hopeless," she whispered. "You did such a great job at the diner, and if someone like you can't deliver, then…"

"No! Nothing's ever hopeless." Man, he'd sent the wrong message this time. "Kristin, even cold cases have been solved twenty years later."

"Twenty years! The bastard who hurt her is still free, walking our streets. We don't have twenty years."

She reached for his hands with both of hers. "For my daughter's sake, I have no pride. In the last two days, she's made real progress, but there's such a long way to go. She refuses to go to school. She refuses to see her friends. She refuses to live in our house. I keep thinking that if the perp was caught, she'd know she was safe. But they've stopped looking for him."

Rick doubted it. "How do you know that?"

"I call all the time, and they have nothing to say. I think they'd like me to stop bothering them."

She raised her face to his, her blue eyes shadowed. "Can you help us? Can you at least make some phone calls? Maybe they'd listen to you more than to me."

He looked at Ashley, now playing fetch with the dog. She waved at him, then threw her stick again for Quincy. Every time the dog returned it to her, he took a second to sniff her, kiss her and walk around her. Kristin was right. Quincy had put them all to shame. The dog was doing his job without being told.

Rick tilted his head back and stared at the cloudless blue sky. He was here for R & R. To relax, to explore a new future. To get away from police work. He needed to mind his own business.

Kristin didn't understand. To her, it was just a few telephone calls. But once he picked up that receiver and dialed, he was into it deep. Especially with another jurisdiction. Captain Stein would either go nuts or he'd cheer. Probably the latter. And the shrink? Hell, who knew what he'd do, what reports he'd write. Technically, Rick was still on the force.

He looked from mother to daughter and back again. Kristin's discouragement saddened him. And little

Ashley would need more support than even Quincy could provide. He'd worked with child victims many times with some success, so how could he ignore these two ladies?

But what if he screwed up again? Another little girl was dead because of him. Perspiration dampened his skin. But he wasn't negotiating this time. Never again. All Kristin was asking him to do was to make a few phone calls. So that was all he'd do. He wouldn't get personally involved with a child victim. Not ever again.

He took a deep breath. "Tell me everything you know," he said quietly. "I'll see what I can find out."

"Thank you so much," she breathed. "I can't tell you what this means to me, to Ashley—"

"Don't get all emotional on me," he ordered. "Or— or I'm outta here."

She sucked it up. A regular lioness. Ashley was lucky.

HIS WALL OF DEFENSE had been smashed after the failed hostage negotiation, and he hadn't had enough time to rebuild it. Despite his effort to remain aloof, he was haunted by Kristin's pain, Ashley's mischievous face, her innocence. All day, his emotions had seesawed between sorrow for Ash, fury at the perp and disappointment in the system that hadn't allowed the case to be solved. By evening, he needed a break.

On the back screened porch, Rick picked up his sax and started with the early days of Charlie Parker. Soon conscious thought disappeared, and he was in another world where only the music mattered. He scooted up in time to some classic Stan Getz— "Where or When," "Time After Time"—and then tried to get into Coltrane's very complicated fingering. It became a practice session for him. Good for his mind. Good for his heart. Good for his soul. Good for auditions.

Music was on his list of possible careers, but something niggled at him. It was probably silly. Even stupid. But he worried about turning his passion into a regular job. For him, the music was personal. It was his joy. Sometimes playing the sax lifted his spirits, sometimes the music simply channeled any emotion he was feeling. At the end of day, it relaxed him. That had been especially true during his days on the force.

He'd once known a woman who enjoyed home decorating. She'd had a talent for it and helped her friends dress up their apartments. Then she quit her office job and became a pro. Exhausted, stressed, she hated it. The joy was gone.

And he sure didn't want to become another Mr. Tanner, the guy in the Harry Chapin song. Mr. Tanner was a dry cleaner with a beautiful voice—until, urged by his friends, he performed at Carnegie Hall and got pelted by the music critics. He never sang again. He lost out both professionally and personally.

Rick clutched his sax. His heart broke for that guy, fiction or not.

Nah, he wouldn't start out at the clubs. He'd start with writing a résumé. He'd write one tomorrow. Then he'd go online and browse. Maybe a private investigation firm needed someone. Maybe he should work temp jobs, try them out until he found one that fit. No commitment. He started to smile. Now, that idea made sense.

He put the mouthpiece to his lips again. Where was

the flute tonight? Maybe his secret partner had simply been passing through, a guest of someone. He played some more, until his eyelids drooped, and he knew he'd sleep well that night.

The next morning, Rick let Quincy out for his bathroom ritual and got ready for their usual run around the lake. When he went outside, however, the dog was gone. Quincy was better trained than that. Losing no time, Rick jogged toward Kristin's house. Sure enough, Ashley was on the side of the road in front of her house, with her feet an inch from the blacktop. The dog stood in front of her, not letting her move.

"Hey, Ash," Rick said casually as he approached. "What are you doing up so early?"

Her sweet smile could melt his heart. "I was waiting for Quincy. He's my best friend now."

Oh, baby...

"Where's Mom?"

"Sleeping." She put her arms around the dog.

From the corner of his eye, he saw the door open and a petite figure appear on the Goldmans' front porch. Immediately, he heard, "Ash-ley!" A note of desperation registered in the call. Kristin spotted them and waved them over.

"Uh-oh." The kid gulped and ran toward her.

He and Quincy followed more slowly and arrived in time to hear Kristin talk about rules of behavior. And scaring Ashley's poor old mother.

Then she added, "And furthermore, you can't bother Rick all the time."

"But I'm not bothering Rick. I'm bothering Quincy!"

Kristin's complexion turned pink. But Rick laughed,

the kind of laugh that reduced a person's blood pressure. "Ash, you're funny. Too funny."

The kid beamed. Kristin watched them, her gaze moving from Rick to her daughter and back again.

"Ashley sure loves Quincy. I don't suppose he's for sale, by any chance?"

"No." No elaboration needed.

"Well, does he have a brother?"

This woman didn't give up. "I don't think so, Kristin. But Ash is welcome to play with him anytime she wants, except early in the morning."

He turned his attention to the child. "To stay healthy, Quincy needs his exercise, so we run every day before it gets too hot outside."

Ash pivoted toward Kristin. "You told me that, Mom. Remember? About big dogs and their strength. You were right."

"Well, whaddayaknow? Your mom was right—for once."

Both of them giggled, and to Rick's great surprise, he joined in. Seemed he was laughing a lot more than usual lately while hanging around these ladies. A nice, temporary diversion.

THEIR ELECTRICITY had been restored the night before, and now Kristin examined the contents of her fridge and cupboards and started a shopping list. Ashley looked up from the book she was reading.

"Please, Mom, can we buy doggy treats, too?"

"Absolutely. And we'll write Quincy's name on the box in big bright letters."

"Good, but dogs see in black and white, and they

can't read." The child left her chair and hugged Kristin. "I love you, Mommy."

She held her daughter tightly in her arms. "And I love you, Ash. Forever and ever. No matter what."

"I know." Ashley leaned into Kristin farther and sighed a big sigh, a weighty sigh.

"What is it, Ash? What are you thinking about?"

"Nothing."

But Kristin knew better. "Everything will be all right, sweetheart. One day, we'll be home again, and—"

"No! We can't. We have to stay here."

Where it's safe.

The unspoken words hung in the air, piercing a veil for Kristin. She now understood that they'd *never* be able to return home as long as Ashley was afraid. Too bad life wasn't a movie where you could reshoot a horrible scene.

"You'll have a lot to tell Dr. Kaplan tomorrow," Kristin said, deciding to change the subject.

"Yes—all about Quincy!" Ashley beamed at her, looking confident and happy.

The dog was the talisman. The key. But one day, Quincy and Rick would disappear. Morningstar Lake was just a summer retreat for most people, including him. And when that happened, Ashley would be devastated again.

Oh, no. Not if Kristin could prevent it. She'd joked with Rick that very morning about Quincy having a brother, but now she had some serious research to do. Private research. On dogs. Particularly German shepherds. Was Quincy unique? Or was he typical of the breed? She'd never owned a dog. She knew nothing about the care, feeding or training of one, but she could learn.

Her daughter deserved all the help and love she needed to recover from her ordeal. Even if that love had to come from a four-legged friend. And even if that four-legged friend had more influence than a mother.

"Come on, Ash. Let's buy some treats."

KRISTIN AND ASHLEY returned home an hour later to find a note on their door.

Quincy wants to play with Ashley.
Come on over. Bring appetites.

"Ooh, Mom. He misses me! Let's go."

"After we unpack…unless you want to walk over by yourself?"

Ashley's eyes grew big. "On the road?"

"I can watch you from the front porch."

The girl shook her head.

"Then let's unpack quickly."

The properties were only about a hundred yards apart, with another house between them. Ashley's reaction to her suggestion reinforced Kristin's earlier thoughts. A dog might help.

Ten minutes later, they knocked on Rick's screen door and heard him call, "Come on in."

Quincy greeted them first. He sniffed Kristin, but stuck with Ashley. And then Rick seemed to fill up the hallway.

"I've got burgers ready for the grill in the back."

"We brought some ice cream for later." Kristin handed him the package.

"Well, thanks, but you didn't have to do that, especially when I've got a favor to ask you."

A favor. Was that the reason for the invite?

"I have a favor, too," said Ashley. "Can me and Quincy go outside? No—wait. Can Quincy and I go outside?"

"Sure, whatever you want," said Rick, glancing at Kristin. "Uh—if it's okay with your mom."

"Good save," she said as her daughter and pal headed toward the back door. She followed Rick into the kitchen, where he stored the ice cream in the freezer, and then continued with him to the porch.

"Would you like a glass of wine, Kristin? I've got Chardonnay or Merlot. Or would you prefer a cold beer?"

His voice was deep, bass deep. A man's voice. She'd gotten used to the soprano pitch around her house, but she'd missed hearing those low tones very much.

"The Chardonnay will hit the spot," she said. "Thank you." She couldn't remember the last time a man had offered her a glass of wine.

He poured the pale liquid into two long-stemmed glasses and handed her one. "Here's to a productive summer for all of us and a welcome to my lovely new neighbors."

She felt herself blush as she touched her glass to his. "That was very nice. But you don't fool me. What was the favor you needed?"

His grin made butterflies dance the tango in her stomach. Attractive didn't begin to describe him. He searched a table with some papers and a laptop on it. Finally, he found what he wanted and handed it to her.

"What do you think of this résumé? I've been working almost all day on it."

Kristin was happy to do him a favor for a change.

Luckily, she'd reviewed more than a few CVs at work, since U.S. Life Corporation was growing rapidly and her department seemed to have an endless need for new junior accountants.

She started to read and felt her jaw drop. "Holy Toledo, Rick. You can't have a dozen objectives on one résumé. It's too murky. A 'jack-of-all-trades' just doesn't work. Who's going to hire someone who doesn't know what he wants?"

"Well, I don't know. But I'm betting someone will hire me. I'm good."

"You're a good cop. I saw that. Let's drop the objective. Put a small background summary on top instead. Maybe three sentences, no more. And then get right to your experience and education."

She started to read those sections. And reread them. "Are you sure you want to leave the department? You've accomplished so much. Four promotions, team leader, awards…"

"Hey, I thought you hated the boys in blue."

"I might be convinced to change my mind." She smiled at him. "I'm not kidding about your experience. Let's see…have you considered going to law school?"

"No, ma'am. That's three years of cracking books. And a lot of money to pay for it."

"Consider it an investment."

"It's still three years of sitting in a classroom, and that's not me. I prefer some action. We need to think of something else. Say, what do you do in that insurance company?"

"Nothing dangerous. In fact, I calculate the dangers

other people face—people such as cops. I'm an actuarial accountant."

She stood up, hands on her hips. "Now, no changing the subject. Rick Cooper, are you telling me you don't know what you want to be when you grow up?"

"Look who's talking! You, sweet Kristin, don't even *look* like a grown-up. Ponytail, jeans, sneakers. Are you sure you're Ashley's mother?"

As if on cue, Ashley's voice rang out. "Mom, can we go to the lake by ourselves?"

She and Rick turned toward the two friends. "Will he stay with her the whole time, not jump in for a swim or something?" she asked Rick quietly.

"He'll stay with her. Let her go, Kristin."

She nodded. "Have fun, sweetheart."

She watched the pair's progress to the lake. "Ashley's so brave with him… She talks to him nonstop. It's as if he's working magic with her. And he's just a dog! I wish…I wish…"

Rick knew exactly what she wished for, and how to make her feel better. Taking her hand, he gently tugged. "Come sit down for a minute."

He enjoyed the way her hand fit in his. Soft. Unresisting. Trusting. He enjoyed it too much. At this particular moment, she didn't seem to have an issue with this particular cop. Unfortunately, he was glad. And that was a warning to him to be vigilant and not get too involved with her and her daughter.

"Quincy and I," he began quietly after they were seated, "have seen lots of kids like Ashley at the Children's Crisis Center in New York."

Her fingers tightened around his. He had her full attention.

"He's a therapy dog, Kristin. We're a volunteer team. The kids at the center have been abused, sexually or physically, or both. Quincy sensed Ashley's distress, and that's why he's so good with her."

"But…but how…?"

He shrugged. "I don't know how he does it. No one really understands why certain dogs are perfect for this work. All prospective canine volunteers are tested for temperament. They have to be suited for working with children. No question about that. Quincy got high marks. The highest in his group."

"I've heard of pet therapy, of course," said Kristin, "at nursing homes and hospitals…."

"At the crisis center, the dogs—somehow—help the kids relax, especially during their first visit. They do it in a way that no person can. Not even their moms and dads." He paused, then added, "Understand what I'm saying?"

"I've been thinking of getting a dog, too."

"You've already got one. Right there." He glanced in the direction Ashley and Quincy had gone. "But my point is that parents can't do it alone. Quincy's simply part of the team."

He watched her absorb his message, hoping he'd gotten through.

"It's silly of me to feel a little jealous, I know…but a mother always thinks she can fix everything. That it's her job—to fix everything." She squeezed both his hands. "Thanks for sharing Quincy's background with me. I feel better. But realistically, he's only a temporary fix. We won't be here forever."

"Let's adopt the one-day-at-a-time philosophy. It's working for me right now."

She stood quickly, knocking her chair over, her face glowing with excitement. "I have an idea."

He got to his feet and waited.

"Maybe you can attach a computer chip to Quincy's ear so we can hear what she's telling him."

The woman watched too many television shows. "You know, Kris, technology is great, but it doesn't replace people skills. There's a good chance she'll discover the chip. She'll resent being spied on. In my opinion, you and her therapist will succeed with her without risking her trust."

"Do you really think so? That we'll succeed? Sometimes, I'm afraid that I'm making mistakes. Should I have insisted she return to school, insisted she see her friends, follow her usual routines at home? But she was paralyzed with fear. You should have seen her...."

He cupped her cheek. "Look at me, Kris. Believe my words. I think Ashley is very lucky to have you in her corner. You're a strong and loving mother."

Color stained her face, and she turned away from him. "Thank you," she whispered. "Thank you very much for such wonderful compliments."

"You're welcome." She deserved those compliments and more. He admired her strength. And she was cute enough to make him stand at attention, which he felt himself doing right now. But she was not the type for a mindless summer fling, and he couldn't deny his disappointment. Although he considered himself open to new relationships, a meaningful one with Kristin was out. He wasn't getting personally involved, she wasn't his responsibility and he wasn't up to "saving" anyone else. So he'd settle for being neighborly. A simple friendship where he could keep a casual eye on her and Ashley.

CHAPTER FOUR

EARLY MONDAY MORNING, Kristin tucked her cell phone into her purse and locked the door behind her. She'd promised Ashley they'd make the round trip to the city in one day—a lot of driving but worth the effort. She'd also mentioned it to Rick the night before. After a week of daily contact, she couldn't disappear without a word. She glanced at her daughter, who seemed cheerful and less reluctant to visit Dr. Kaplan this time.

They'd been at Morningstar Lake for exactly two weeks now, and maybe Ash had a lot to say to the therapist. Hmm…perhaps "say" was finally becoming the right word, although Ash still avoided all reference to the attack. On the bright side, her daughter was participating in conversations when she was spoken to directly. Kristin wondered how the psychologist and Ash would make out that day.

Behind the wheel, she reminded herself to focus on the road. The countryside was spectacular. Tall oaks, foliage-covered hills, picturesque farms with their traditional red barns and wooden gates, clusters of cows in the meadows. Beautiful. Maybe one day, she and Ash could have a summer home here. Her heart lightened. Dreaming helped.

"Lunch before or after?" They were approaching the city now, and Kristin glanced at her daughter, who seemed to be dozing.

Ash opened her eyes, however, and said, "After. But in a restaurant. Not at our house."

No surprise, but at this rate, they'd never get back home. Kristin could guess at the threats the perp had made—he'd track Ashley down, he'd hurt her mother, he knew where she lived. Child victims, however, did not communicate like adults, and Ashley had been unconscious when found. When she regained consciousness, she chose not to speak. So Kristin and her daughter had never had an in-depth conversation about the incident.

Kristin had read a ton of material on child molestation and had been on the phone with advocates from the Sexual Assault Crisis Center from the beginning. They'd given her a list of psychiatric specialists to consider, and that's how she'd found Sheila Kaplan.

They crossed the Triborough Bridge and headed toward Queens on the way to Long Island. "I wonder where Rick lives," she said casually. "I know he's in the city."

"Bayside."

"How'd you learn that?"

"Quincy told me."

Kristin almost slammed into the car ahead of her when the driver braked at that moment. "Quincy told you?" she asked in a strangled voice. Maybe they'd both lose their minds before long.

"Not in *English,* Mom," Ash said with exaggerated patience.

Please, God, not dog language. "In Spanish?" She tried to lighten her voice.

Ash giggled.

Her tension disappeared as though she were a rubber band that suddenly snapped.

"Rick tells Quincy stuff and Quincy tells me."

"Like where they live?"

Ash nodded.

"What else?"

"Umm…cats. Quincy chases cats. Especially Butterscotch, who lives upstairs. She winds up in a tree."

"Dogs chasing cats is an old story."

"Maybe. But Quincy would rather be with me than Butterscotch. I just know it." Ashley looked at Kristin now, her eyes gleaming. "You know what, Mom? I'm so happy that Aunt Marsha loaned us her house. I'm so happy that Rick and Quincy live near us. Rick is so nice. He kids around. I really like him."

Quite a voluntary mouthful. "Do you like him better than Quincy?"

"No! Quincy comes first."

Kristin winked at her daughter. "After moms, of course."

"I love you the best, Mommy."

She squeezed Ashley's knee. "I know, sweetheart. I know."

"And I wish we could stay at the lake forever."

Her daughter had the last word, but Kristin's heart ached for her. Ashley's solution was unrealistic. As much as Kristin loved the country, too, someday…was not today.

THIRTY MINUTES INTO Ashley's session with her therapist, Dr. Kaplan emerged from her office and closed the door behind her. Smiling, she approached Kristin.

"Excellent progress, Mrs. McCarthy. A real break-through with her verbal communication, even though she hasn't yet broached the 'elephant.'" The woman squeezed Kristin's hand. "She wants to share something with you—some really great work. Wait until you see."

Kristin could have sworn sunlight filled the room at exactly that moment. She jumped to her feet.

"Before we go in," continued Dr. Kaplan, "keep in mind our discussions about progress and how it's often made in fits and starts. Remember that every child is unique. So we'll have to see where this goes. We'll take our lead from Ashley."

So there was a little cloud along with the sunshine. But sometimes Kristin just needed to live in the moment. And this day was getting better and better.

She followed the young psychologist into her work-place, which resembled a playroom more than a tradi-tional office. Although there were framed credentials, a desk, file drawers and a computer, Dr. Kaplan also had two tables, several chairs, and bookcases filled with dolls, games, toys and clay, which took up most of the space.

Ash sat at one of the tables, art supplies at hand. Even from a distance, Kristin could see her daughter's rendition of Quincy, taking up an entire large sheet of drawing paper. She'd written the dog's name beneath the picture.

"This is great, Ash. He looks like the real thing." She'd often wondered if musical talent and artistic ability went hand in hand. The depiction of the silver-black shepherd was truly excellent.

But Ashley was now immersed in a second project on a different piece of paper, in colored pencils. She motioned Kristin closer, and then continued to work. A city street. A long building, two stories high. People walking in front. An entrance with big glass doors…big display windows…people going inside…beyond the doors a marquee….

Kristin bit her lip, her hands clenched. She easily recognized the depiction.

Perspiration dotted Ashley's forehead and face as she worked. Finally, she thrust the sheet at Kristin. "There!"

The mall. In detail, from the outside. It was *their* mall, not any old mall. The movie theater had posters on the left side of the entrance where Kristin had dropped Ash off that day.

"Ash! This is fantastic work. You're amazing. I'm so proud of you." Maybe this was another breakthrough.

"I think the country air agrees with you," said Dr. Kaplan, smiling and closely examining the picture.

Ashley smiled back. "I like it at the lake."

"Because…?" prompted the doctor.

"It's safe." An instant reply. No hesitation.

Ashley's hands were in motion once again, fingers on the table, moving as though on a piano keyboard. She hummed under her breath. Kristin recognized the piece. Beethoven's "Für Elise." Her daughter could go through the entire piece without a break when she was only six. John had called her amazing and had proudly taken full credit for it!

Kristin glanced at the psychologist. The doc smiled. "A very good day's work," the therapist said.

Kristin nodded, then kissed Ash on the forehead. "We need to go now, sweetheart. Dr. Kaplan has to help other children, too."

Ash nodded but said, "I have to finish," and kept "playing."

"How about continuing at our house?" A baby grand sat in their living room, a library of sheet music next to it in a cabinet.

"No!" Her hands stilled. "It's not safe." She reached for her illustration of Quincy and added words after his name. Now the caption read "Quincy Knows Everything."

Kristin wished she could speak dog language. She searched the doctor's face, then walked to the far end of the room. The therapist followed. "We have the lake house until August 1. Will we be able to go home by then?"

Dr. Kaplan, practicing psychologist with advanced degrees, simply said, "I don't know."

Kristin's stomach cramped. She and Ash were living on her savings now and if she didn't return to work in August, she'd lose her job entirely. Unemployment was simply not an option…yet neither was disappointing Ashley. Kristin was caught squarely between the two priorities, with no idea how she was going to resolve the dilemma.

RICK PACED his front porch on the evening of his neighbors' trip to the city. He glanced at his wristwatch every ten seconds in the light of the overhead fixture. It was nine o'clock, fully dark outside, and now he was concerned the way a good neighbor would be. By his calculations, they should have been home a long time ago. Three hours in, three hours back, an hour with the therapist, an hour for lunch. He'd found himself checking the time since about five o'clock and had even seasoned a beautiful sirloin for the grill. The meat was still marinating in his fridge. He'd staved off his own hunger pains with a can of soup.

It wasn't that he and Kristin had made arrangements to meet back here for dinner. They hadn't. The ladies didn't report to him, nor were they in his caseload. Damn. Was that how he saw them? He took a moment and put his mind at ease. No, they were strictly neighbors. Ashley's situation belonged elsewhere.

He looked at his watch again. Maybe they'd gone shopping. Maybe Kristin had diverted Ashley's attention to new clothes. Bathing suits and summer stuff. Or, even better, Kristin might have talked Ash into visiting friends. Yeah. That would be great if it were true. He could live with that as a reason for delay, but not for staying out overnight. Kristin had definitely mentioned returning to Morningstar Lake this evening. She would have let him know if she'd changed her mind. Wouldn't she?

He touched his cell phone, ready to call her, when Quincy rose from the ground, barked softly and walked to the edge of the steps, staring intently toward the road. Rick saw nothing but the night, heard nothing but insects humming, but felt himself relax. The dog was never wrong. And…there! Another bull's-eye. The headlights of a slow-moving vehicle twinkled among the trees as it wended its way closer. Rick tracked it and nodded in approval. Slow and steady in the darkness on unfamiliar country roads.

He met them in their driveway, Quincy at his side. When he opened Kristin's door, he saw Ash sound asleep in the passenger seat.

"Welcome home," he whispered, reaching for Kristin's hand and helping her out of the car. "I was getting a bit concerned."

Tired blue eyes began to focus. "You were?"

"Yes." He pointed at his watch. "Look at the time."

Standing now, she leaned against the vehicle and yawned. "I didn't know I had a curfew, Pops."

He'd blown it. Now he'd back off.

But then she smiled and said, "We had a great afternoon and a lousy evening on the road."

He didn't like the sound of the last part, and although that sweet smile of hers raised his temperature, it didn't deflect his focus.

"Explain lousy evening. What happened? Where were you? Who else was there? Can you describe—"

"Huh? Slow down. What are you talking…? Ohh, now I get it," she said. "You're back in cop mode. Well, let's see…what happened was car trouble. We were at McDonald's. Lots of diners. Two golden arches…" She dimpled up at him. "But we're fine, Rick. Thanks for caring."

More heat. The scorching kind. That mouth…he wanted to kiss her. He stroked her cheek instead. "I'm glad you're both safe at home."

She didn't move. Her glance lingered on him, her expression thoughtful, questioning…eager? Warning bells rang in his head. He was glad they were safe, but that was all he'd meant.

He moved away. "So, tell me about the car," he said, getting back to the real business.

"It wouldn't start. I called the AAA for help."

"Battery?"

She shook her head. "The doohickies were dirty." She made a small circling motion with her fingers. "The terminals. The guy used a steel brush. I could have done it myself—if I'd known what was wrong. I waited almost an hour and they fixed it in five minutes."

"Take a class," he suggested. "Most adult education programs offer classes in auto mechanics every fall and spring."

She glanced at her daughter. "I'll think about it— later." She pointed at the house. "I'll be right back. Would you stay with her?"

Rick nodded, and Kristin disappeared with her purse and a shopping bag. He gazed inside the car and studied the sleeping girl. Kris had described her as an outgoing kid, a good student with lots of friends. He'd seen some of that himself, so Kristin's assessment had been pretty objective—for a mom. But their lives had been turned upside down by a stinking perp.

He felt his anger start to brew again. Kristin's gentle child lived in fear and worked hard to cover it up in order to keep going each day. Kristin's tiny family had been damaged, first by the death of her husband, and then by Ashley's…experience. Two life-altering events hitting within a short period. His muscles rippled, his fists tightened. Suddenly, he was happy to involve himself in Ashley's case.

"Hi, Quincy!" a young voice, a sleepy voice, called.

The dog had already taken over the driver's seat, probably sensing Ash would awaken.

"Hey, Ash," said Rick. "You're home."

She smiled at him, then turned her head in all directions. "Where's Mom?" she asked quickly.

"In the house. And we're with you because you were still asleep."

"Oh, okay." She hugged and cooed to Quincy, totally at one with the dog. The kid was a sweetheart.

Kristin returned and Ashley got out of the car, the shepherd following her.

"Time for a real bed," Kristin said.

"I guess." Ashley looked longingly at Quincy.

Kristin kissed her daughter on the forehead. "We had a terrific day. One of the best. Don't you think?"

The girl actually did pause to consider her answer. "Yes," she finally pronounced. "We did have a good day. But we're not going back home."

"Not for a while yet, honey."

"Never. We just can't."

"We'll see…"

Rick intervened. "How about taking Quincy inside for a visit, Ashley? He's missed you. If he follows your commands, you can give him a treat."

She raised a fist in salute. "Yes!" And the two disappeared.

Neither adult spoke for a moment.

"Maybe I should call a real estate agent," Kristin whispered. "We can't stay here forever. The therapist didn't promise Ash would be over this by August. But we could move to another neighborhood in Mayfield, or even to another town. That might help her get back on track."

He put his arm around her, strictly for comfort. "Ashley will improve, Kris. She's already made great strides here, and one day she'll laugh and talk on the phone with all her old friends until you threaten to take it away."

"Promise?"

"I've seen it happen—and not just once."

"Thank you," she murmured, "for giving me hope." She ran inside and a minute later, Quincy reappeared.

No question about it. Kristin deserved some assistance. Rick was going to nose around this case and try to find the SOB who'd hurt Ashley. And if he needed some big brass behind him, he'd give Stein a call.

The irony didn't escape him.

RICK STARTED HIS RESEARCH the next morning with calls to two buddies in Nassau County, Long Island, Kristin's home turf. Andy Wheeler and Dave Evans were seasoned pros who knew how to listen even when no one was talking. Moreover, they'd keep their own mouths shut. Rick trusted them. Too bad he'd had to leave messages. Law enforcement ran nonstop, 24/7. They were busy.

He tucked his cell phone in his pocket, packed his fishing gear and motioned to the dog. Outside, the sky was clear. No surprise storms today.

He drove first to Dora's Diner for a quick breakfast and a packed lunch to go, and saw Sam Keaton at the counter, draining a cup of coffee.

"Got a minute?" asked Rick, after placing his order. He nodded at a corner booth.

"For you—sure." The older man followed him down the aisle. "Find a new job yet?"

"Still working on it," replied Rick. "My résumé is coming along. Kristin looked it over, gave me some suggestions."

"Well, she can't change the experience section. With your excellent record, she must have been impressed— and confused about you wanting to leave the NYPD."

The man was so transparent. Rick glared at him. "It's not going to happen, Sam. I'm out. However…" He felt his neck get warm, then his face. "What more can you tell me about Ashley McCarthy?"

"So the kid got to you, huh?" asked the sheriff, lowering his voice. They faced each other across the table, and Rick understood from his concerned expression that he would share what he knew.

But in the next moment, Sam smiled and leaned forward. "Perhaps it was the mother who got to you?" The older man chuckled as though he'd cracked the funniest joke in the world.

Sam would share, all right, when he was good and ready.

Rick sighed loudly and waited. He knew his friend. More was coming.

He was correct.

"I knew you'd come alive again," said Sam. "The job can wear you down, that's for sure. You just needed to come home to Morningstar Lake and catch your breath."

Rick leaned forward. "I am *not* on the job, Sam. I'm not going back to the job. I'm just asking as a long-time friend—what do you know about the status of the Ashley McCarthy case?"

His smile disappeared. "I know what Kristin McCarthy told me the day they arrived at the lake. I know what Marsha Goldman told me on the phone." The sheriff spoke softly again.

Rick raised his hand in a halting motion. "Why did Kristin come to you?"

"To tell me the Long Island police knew she was here with her daughter—she's kept them informed of her status since the attack. She asked to be notified if they called us." Sam paused, but seemed to have more on his mind. "The case is getting cold—it's been over two months."

Rick nodded. "Kristin thinks we're all a bunch of incompetent morons." In his case, she might be right.

"She's the mom. She wants answers. And there is an official investigation in their hometown," said Sam. "Mayfield, Long Island. But basically, I know nothing because the officers downstate know nothing. The kid was unconscious when they arrived and later on wouldn't speak, wouldn't draw, wouldn't reveal anything about the perp." He lowered his voice further. "She was found on the floor of the men's room, clothes ripped off, bruised and...bleeding."

Rick sucked air. Felt sweat pop out all over his body. And saw blood. Red droplets splattered on a white blouse. A little girl. Was Ashley wearing a white blouse that day?

"I lost a kid, Sam!" The words exploded in a harsh whisper. His head dropped into his hands. "And the parents. The father shot them—we were right outside the house." *Bang. Bang. Bang.*

Doc Romano might be the best, but Rick had known Sam for thirty years, since Rick was five years old. He'd trust the man with his life...and with his soul.

"Damnation!" Sam's hand fisted on the table. "I figured something like that, but I'm sorry to be right. No wonder you're at a crossroad. You're a mess."

Rick grunted. "Perfect description."

A beat of time passed, and Sam spoke once more. "Sometimes, Detective, that invisible armor we wear breaks down. The cop disappears and the human being emerges. You're just being human right now. And what's wrong with that? You've been thrown over the edge once too often."

The sheriff's words resonated. Rick's armor had cracked. And he'd suffered. Was still suffering.

"It's an unsettling business we're in," Sam continued. "An unsettling business."

Rick laughed, surprised he was able to appreciate Sam's dry humor. "That's an understatement."

"Maybe. But it helps me put the job into perspective. Makes it doable."

And somehow, for twelve years, Rick had been doing the job and loving it. Just this morning he'd thought he could take on Ashley's case without a second thought. Well, he'd been proved wrong. His memories still haunted him. And if he couldn't handle kids' cases, what good was he? He glanced at his old friend.

"This unsettling business has an unsettled officer, Sam. And right now I'd appreciate your help with Ashley."

"You got it." He reached for his pen and wrote on a napkin. "My contact is Joe Silva. Start with him. Mention my name or not—use your own judgment. Conduct your own investigation."

Rick had already started, by calling his buddies. The anxiety that had been his faithful companion since the shootings began to ease. A peaceful feeling slowly settled within him as he faced the truth. His truth. He hadn't returned to the lake only for the fishing. Or for the isolation. Or for the cool evenings or the hiking. He'd returned for Sam. For absolution.

His plans wouldn't change. He just needed to forgive himself for making mistakes. Fatal ones. Not an easy task.

"Sorry, Quince," he said, scratching the dog behind the ears, "but as good as you are, sometimes you're just not enough."

Ashley's image popped into his head. The little girl and her mom were struggling. He wanted to help.

But helping Kristin would be the last piece of police work he'd ever do.

CHAPTER FIVE

HOPE REMAINED HIGH in Kristin's heart the day after their trip to the city. Ash had asked to visit the music store in town just to browse through their classical sheet music—if they had any. She was having trouble remembering the fingering for the first movement of Beethoven's Sonata *Pathétique,* but could work it out on a table or a desk if she had the notation. She didn't need to hear the real music out loud. She played it in her head.

It sounded crazy, and anyone else would think Ash weird, but Kristin believed her daughter. Ashley heard the music in her mind just like her father had. When he slept, John had said, his dreams were lush with melody and harmony. Sometimes he'd heard full orchestral arrangements and sometimes a solo violin. He'd said that Ashley's talent would be larger than his, but they should follow her lead in how hard to push her. All musical styles were acceptable. He wanted her to explore and to enjoy.

John had stepped back when Ash was five, and hired a teacher known for working with young children. Ash galloped ahead, learning and playing as though it were a game, and grinning like the Cheshire cat when she mastered her material. Of course, listening to music nurtured her talent, too.

The progress had never stopped until now. Lessons were on hold indefinitely, and at this point, Kristin would once again allow Ashley to take the lead in this area of her life.

Kris drove down Main Street. She passed the library they'd visited, and searched for Tri-County Music. It was hard to miss. A brightly lit neon guitar shone in the window, and she wondered if the store had a classical section at all. Of course, this effort would be unnecessary if she'd been able to go to their home and get Ashley's own music collection.

She turned to her daughter. "What do you think?"

"They don't make money on kids like me."

"You cracked a joke! That's so cool." Kristin unsnapped her seat belt and gave Ash a quick hug. "Come on, my little capitalist, let's see if we can contribute something to their bottom line."

Inside, the store was much larger than it seemed from the street. It ran deep from front to back. Drums and guitars took up a lot of floor space, saxophones and trumpets hung on the walls, but racks of CDs and sheet music had a big section, too. Signs on the cashier's desk proclaimed Inquire about Summer Rentals and Practice Rooms.

"I bet lots of parents rent practice rooms for their drummers." Kristin chuckled.

Ash smiled while thumbing through some sheet music. After a minute or two, she sighed in disappointment. "It's all pop stuff that I can play on my own. They don't have what I need."

Kristin wasn't ready to give up. "Let's ask." She caught the eye of a young clerk, who quickly walked over. Kristin explained their quest.

"Sure," he said, leading them to the end of the rack. "Classical stuff is right here. We've got all the great composers. Browse all you want." He smiled up at Kristin. "Are you a music teacher?"

"No. This is for my daughter."

The teenager glanced at Ashley. "No problem. We have easy arrangements of the classics, too."

"Oh, no." Kristin began to explain his mistake, but then sensed Ashley's reaction. Her stillness. Her anger. She saw her daughter's normally pale complexion whiten to alabaster as the child tilted her head back to stare the boy in the face.

Kristin's heart picked up speed. *That's my girl! Be brave. Look him in the eye and tell him what you want.* She kept silent, but stepped closer to her daughter.

Ash, however, moved away from her and declared, "I want Beethoven's Sonata No. 8 Opus 13 in C Minor. I want Debussy's 'Clair de Lune,' and as for Bach— that's Johann Sebastian—any minuet you have in the store. And I want every one of them in the original notation." She put her hands on her narrow hips and said, as if to an errant pupil, "That means the composer's actual work."

The clerk held up his hands, palms outward. "Don't bite my head off. How would I know? Here's the rack of sheet music. Take as much time as you want, and I'll see what we've got in the back."

Kristin watched the interchange, riveted. Then Ash reached out for her. A thin blue vein throbbed at her temple. Red blotches stained her cheeks and beads of perspiration dotted her forehead. "I don't feel so good." She began to sway.

Kristin grabbed her around the waist and desperately looked for a chair. "Take a deep breath. You're going to be fine, baby." She *had* to be fine. "You were great. Just great. Now breathe."

The employee rolled a chair to them. "Is she getting sick?"

Kristin beamed. "Because of your unintended insult, she's never been better. I owe you. Thank you very much."

This incident was another step forward. Definitely worthy of a journal entry.

Even better, she'd share it with Rick.

TEN MINUTES LATER, Kristin rented a practice room. After watching her daughter greedily study the musical scores, reading the mess of black dots as eagerly as Kristin would read a great novel, she plunked down twenty dollars for a half hour of rental time. Not that Ashley had asked her to. She hadn't. But, aside from those brief moments in the library with the dog books, Ash had not been deeply absorbed in anything for two months. Kris thought the time for phantom playing might be over. Maybe it was time for a real keyboard. Twenty bucks might be the best investment she could make for her daughter's sake.

Ashley didn't comment on Kris's decision. She just kept studying the notation while automatically following her mother to the private room in an alcove at the back of the store.

"This is the part, Mom," said Ash, after placing the sheet music on the piano and sitting down. "See? Right here is where I always screw up." She pointed at the Beethoven.

Kristin nodded. "It looks tough." Of course, it *all*

looked tough to a woman whose sole musical contribution to the family was the ability to carry a tune—barely.

She sat on the bench next to her daughter, watching and waiting, and holding her breath. Ashley placed her right hand on the keyboard, and…did nothing. Slowly, her left hand went to her chest and she leaned against Kristin.

"Mommy, I can't," she barely whispered. "I'm scared. *He* hurt me. In here." She tapped the area near her heart. Her eyes darkened, the pupils getting larger, almost filling her face.

Kristin's skin prickled. She embraced her daughter, held her close, not knowing whether "in here" referred to body or soul.

"I know, baby. I know. But you're safe now. You're very safe. I'm with you. Every minute. No one can hurt you, precious girl."

Ashley's gaze became more unfocused. She stared past Kristin to the side wall. "No. Not safe. He'll get us." Her tone was wooden. Flat. A robot's voice. Now she turned forward again and stared unblinkingly ahead. But what did she see?

"It's movie time," said Ashley. "No talking allowed."

Movie time? What did she mean?

Ash closed her eyes and tilted her head as if she were listening hard, then carefully placed her hands on the keyboard and gazed down. Suddenly, she made the piano sing. Ten fingers moved rapidly in a sprightly dance, the music happy, lighthearted…like children skipping. The piece was totally unfamiliar to Kristin. Her child was engaged in her own world. Normal for Ash when she played.

After a minute, however, the music changed and

became slower, quieter. "Shh. It's dark now. No talking allowed," whispered Ashley.

"I wasn't…"

But Ash was deep into her playing, repeating the tranquil theme, which was also unfamiliar to Kristin. When the music changed again, however, Kristin recognized it immediately as the delightful opening number from *Hairspray*, an upbeat song called "Good Morning, Baltimore."

And all the pieces fell into place.

Hairspray had been playing that horrible afternoon. Ash had put herself back in the theater, telling her mother what had happened through music.

"Baltimore" evolved into a quiet march for about eight bars. Enough time to walk to the restroom? Suddenly, thunder crashed, lightning sizzled. Treble and bass warred with each other before colliding in a cacophony of harsh sound. Ashley's arms stretched from one end of the keyboard to the other, her mouth a grimace, her fingers never stopping. She worked it, she lived it, and now she shared it with Kristin.

Including a dirge at the end. Unconsciousness. Perhaps her own death.

When the last note faded, absolute silence filled the room and pounded against Kristin's ears. Her gaze held Ashley's, and she reached for her daughter.

"Thank you, Ash. I think I understand. Thank you so much for telling me."

Ashley wrapped herself around Kristin and rested. "You're welcome. I had to tell you now, but I don't know why," she murmured. "Mom, you're crying!" She brushed at a tear with her finger.

"So are you." Kris held her child, cuddled and kissed her. "I'm so proud of you, Ash. You're amazing. Have I ever told you that you're a fabulous kid?"

"Yes."

"It's the truth," she said. "Another truth is that I didn't recognize most of the music you played."

Ashley started to giggle. "Neither did I."

More discoveries. "Not bad for a beginning composer," she teased. "Daddy would be so proud of you, darling. So proud."

Ashley became silent, then tears pooled again and overflowed. "But do you think he'd still love me?" The question almost choked her.

Stunned, Kristin couldn't answer immediately, and when she did, she was barely coherent. "Still love you? Are you kidding? He'd adore you. He'd love you till the end of time, Ash, no matter what. In fact, he loves you from heaven right now. Daddy and I—our love is forever, unconditional. No matter what. For always."

Ash heaved a big sigh and leaned against her. "I just wanted to make sure."

"Well, now you know...for sure."

At its best, parenthood was a challenge. At its worst, it was a struggle through quicksand.

Once more, Kristin had hope. The last few minutes together had been filled with honest communication—perhaps of an unusual type, but it didn't matter. Ashley had shared her story, her fears, and believed Kristin's responses. Trust was building. Maybe one day the old Ashley, or someone close to her, would be back.

Kristin tapped the sheet music that still rested on the piano. "Are you up to this?"

Ash glanced at her watch. "Do you have enough money for more time?"

"Absolutely. Another half hour is fine." She'd worry about the bill later.

"Then yes. I'd like to play my real pieces. My real music. I used to know everything by memory."

"You probably still do. Take some time and enjoy yourself. I'll wait on the bench just outside the store."

"But lock the door here, okay? I'll feel better if no one can get in."

Kris walked across the room and was barely over the practice room's threshold when the beautiful opening of "Clair de Lune" filled the air. Ash had entered her own world.

Oddly, Kris found no door to the room, or to the other practice rooms in that corridor. However, they were all tucked away from the selling floor and general customers would have no reason to wander here. Ashley would be fine, and Kristin would check on her every ten minutes.

She spoke with the store manager this time, used her credit card, then made her way outdoors, eager to enjoy the sunshine, the lovely breeze—and the knowledge that Ashley had taken another step. Maybe a giant step.

She leaned back on the bench provided for waiting parents, and allowed her lids to drift down and rest. John filled her mind, the remarkable man himself and the pain of losing him. She'd never want to go through that again. Her solitude lasted two full minutes before she heard a vehicle pull to a stop in front of her, and a familiar voice call her name.

Rick jumped from the Honda, leaving Quincy inside with the window half-down. He walked toward her while scanning the street, then pulled off his sunglasses when he reached her.

"Where's Ash?"

Kristin glanced at her watch. "I'll check on her very soon, but she's got almost twenty-five more minutes to go."

"For what?"

"I'm renting a practice room. The sign said to ask, so I did."

"Ahh. And she's practicing the…?"

"Piano. She plays piano." Her statement was quiet and deliberate. She tasted the words, loved the flavor, and then felt a grin bloom on her face.

"What happened, Kris?" His voice was quiet, too, but he glanced toward the doorway and at their surroundings as though searching for cause.

Of course he'd pick up on the change in her voice, in her expression.

"You look…I don't know. Relaxed and happy?" He sounded incredulous, as though he couldn't imagine Kristin totally at ease.

She stood and stepped toward him, glad for the opportunity to share the hope that had taken root. "Something good happened," she admitted. "Actually, two things. But first, Ashley was supremely insulted and—"

"Insulted?" Rick headed for the door. "I'm glad I saw you. My dad asked me to pick up a new music stand, but I'll buy it somewhere else now—after I give them a piece of my mind."

"No! Wait. I didn't explain correctly." She grabbed his wrist, annoyed with herself for delivering the news backward. He might not be a working cop, but man, he was protective.

"She's fine, Rick. Absolutely fine. Would I be out here if she wasn't?"

She saw him take a deep breath. "Start from the beginning," he said.

But a woman exited the store just then, her salt-and-pepper hair pulled high. Her excited gaze landed on Kristin. "Are you the mother of that gifted young pianist? They told me you'd be outside."

"Yes, I am. But—is something wrong?" She'd assured Ashley that no one would bother her. Kristin lurched forward and grabbed the doorknob. "I'd better check on my daughter now. Be right back." She disappeared inside.

Rick followed Kris, the gray-haired woman right behind him. He heard the piano music when he was halfway across the room and saw a silent group of people gathered near the back of the store, which seemed unusual. When Kris made a beeline for the crowd, he slowed his step and listened more closely. Could that really be coming from little Ashley? Did children play Beethoven with that kind of emotion and technique?

He watched Kristin as she stood in the doorway, staring inside, an awed smile on her face. He had his answer. Her child was, indeed, exceptional.

"Who teaches her?" the other woman whispered to him.

"I don't know."

"You're not the father?"

"I'm—I'm a friend. Their closest friend in town." A friend who kept learning more and more about his intriguing neighbors.

Kris tiptoed toward them, her wallet open. "I'm

going to pay for another half hour," she whispered. "I just can't pull her away when she's finally acting like her real self."

Rick covered her hand with his. "My treat. Put your money back."

"I can't let you—"

"Yes, you can. I want to." Just like he wanted to keep her hand in his and pull her close. The money was such a little gesture to make life easier for Kristin.

He went to the cash register, leaving the two women alone. Forty dollars an hour for a practice room was out of sight. A kid like Ashley would probably want to play for hours every day. Kristin could never afford that. His thoughts went into overdrive. He had connections at the clubs…knew musicians he could call….

The piano went silent. The small crowd was buzzing. He saw Kristin rush forward, worry on her face. In two leaps, he was there with her—ahead of her—and through the group of listeners, who were murmuring while they dispersed.

Ash was alone inside.

"What's the—"

The child ran to him before he could finish the sentence. She wrapped her skinny arms tightly around him, and he could feel her quivering like autumn leaves in the wind. He made soothing noises and hugged her close, his glance darting around the small room, bouncing from the walls to ceiling to corners, looking for reasons. But as he'd immediately seen, the place was empty except for the piano and the bench.

"The people, the people." Her voice broke. "They

were listening. So many people. Who are they? I didn't know them. I was alone."

"Aww, Ashley. You were never alone," Rick said. "Your mom would never leave you, and I was right here all the time, too. Listening to your beautiful music. And I'm guessing that's what everyone else was doing."

"But I wanted privacy…."

"I'm sorry, honey," said Kristin.

Ashley wriggled out of Rick's arms and went to her mother, then turned back to him.

"Where's Quincy?" she asked in a trembling voice.

Just as she asked that question, Rick heard a store-wide announcement. "There's a dog going nuts in the Honda Pilot outside. Anyone know him?"

"That's Quincy," exclaimed Ash. "He's upset. He needs me now." And she took off, calling over her shoulder, "Mom, could you buy the music, please?"

"It's always two steps forward and one step back," Kristin said, picking up the sheet music. "There was a moment today when I thought we'd have no more reversals, but I guess that's not realistic."

"She's coming alive, Kris. That's what I see. And birth is painful."

"We came here for a quiet life," said Kristin.

"Quiet is boring."

"So says a cop."

He eyed her steadily. "Ex-cop." He grinned at her. "Hmm…maybe I'll take piano lessons. How's that for a new career?"

Kristin laughed, just the way he liked to see her.

"Your daughter can really kick butt on that keyboard," he said. "She's fabulous."

"Her dad predicted this. Ash is quite the musician. Multiple instruments. So be nice to her, and she might show you a thing or two."

Her husband. Kris hadn't spoken much about him before. "Or maybe," Rick said slowly, "she could be my partner again?"

Kristin cocked her head, her nose wrinkled. "What do you mean?"

He whistled the beginning of "Where or When" and watched her eyes light up.

"Oh. My. God." She laughed with delight. "Truly? You? This is so cool. Wait until Ash finds out. She's going to love you."

Outside again, they saw Ashley, with Quincy at her side, talking to the woman who'd approached them earlier.

"She's so brave, as long as Quincy's with her," murmured Kris, picking up her pace.

"She's showing wisdom."

Ashley made the introductions. "Mrs. Shilling is a piano teacher. She—she wants to work with me."

The woman stepped forward, her hand extended to Kris. "Can we talk?"

Rick looked from Ash to the teacher and back to Ash again. The child was clutching the dog. *Nope. Not ready.*

Kristin put her arm around her daughter. "Ashley needs to be part of the conversation, too."

The kid jumped in. "I'm sorry, Mrs. Shilling. I'm on vacation now."

Vacation? Rick had to laugh to himself. The kid did schoolwork all day. And now she was doing some fancy talking. By the teacher's expression, Rick could tell she thought so, too.

"I see," said the woman, reaching into her purse. "But if you change your mind, or get *bored* on your vacation, playing the same music the same way without improving, just give me a call." She gave a card to both Ashley and Kristin, then shook Kristin's hand and said something to her privately.

Rick watched the lady as she went to her car. Even Ashley tracked her. *Smart woman,* he thought. She'd planted some seeds.

"What did she say to you?" he asked, standing close to Kristin after the teacher was gone. Kris's mouth was hanging open.

"No charge," she whispered. "She said she'd teach Ashley for free." She leaned into him, and he wrapped his arms around her as naturally as if he'd held her a thousand times before.

"Suck it up, partner," he gently chided. She took a deep breath. He was getting used to some emotional displays, not that he could blame her. However, he was used to seeing her control them, too. The lioness was quite a woman.

He'd hunt down a piano for them immediately and pay for the tuning, too. Ashley needed a quality sound.

His cell rang. He connected with one hand while keeping the other arm around Kristin. Dave Evans, returning his earlier call. Great. His pals were coming through. He'd be happy to pass any news on to Kristin— good or bad. But hopefully good.

"I SUPPOSE IF NO NEWS IS good news, then we have good news," said Kristin the next afternoon. Rick and the dog had stopped by with an update, and now the adults were enjoying a cold drink on the back porch while Ashley and Quincy were outside playing.

"But Kris, we have had news," he replied patiently. "I've been assured by two extremely reliable sources that the case is still wide open. It hasn't been pushed aside. No one on your local force has forgotten about Ashley."

"I'm grateful for that, but I guess I was hoping for a catch…you know, what do you call it when the cops get the guy?"

"A collar."

"Yeah. That's it. With the DNA they have, I was hoping, even though I know they would have called me if that had happened."

Unexpectedly, he reached for her hands and enclosed them in his own. "Kris, the DNA doesn't match any registered sex offender in the area…."

She liked his touch, how he pressed her fingers, communicating with her. A tender message of comfort. It had been so long… She refocused on the conversation.

"So maybe a new guy came to town. Maybe he's living there."

"Or maybe he's come and already gone," Rick said. "But whatever the case, Ashley has to move forward— even if the perp is never caught. You know that, Kris."

Now, he was stroking her bare arm. She shivered, then felt hot. *Pathetic.*

She nodded. "That's my goal. And we're trying."

"And that is exactly what I admire about you," he said. "No one is a fiercer mother than a lioness, and when I see you with Ashley, I also hear you roar."

"Oh, my goodness. You're making me emotional again, but I'm sucking it up!" She extracted one of her hands and clasped it over his. "I haven't thanked you yet, Rick, for your time. Your interest. You've been great. I really appreciate all you've done."

He lifted her hand to his mouth and kissed it softly. "You're very welcome, but you can hold the thanks. My next act will be even better!"

KRIS HAD INVITED HIM to stay for dinner, but Rick couldn't postpone his own business any longer. He had a date—a phone date with Doc Romano—every Wednesday at four. And that was that. He wouldn't put it past his C.O. to send a search party if he didn't check in. But a whole hour with the shrink? Talking about what?

When he called, he discovered two things: he could set the topics and the time limit, at least for now. Beautiful.

The shrink was an angler. They talked trout fishing for thirty minutes and Rick's job search for ten. Then they hung up.

Next week, he was supposed to tell the guy how many positions he'd applied for. Piece of cake.

THE FOLLOWING WEEK, Kristin and Ashley visited Dr. Kaplan again. They also received a loaner piano for the living room of their borrowed home—Rick's second act. He'd conjured up the instrument through friends who owned a nightclub, and had also arranged for it to be tuned. It seemed her neighbor hadn't been kidding when he claimed to know most everyone in town.

Marsha and her husband had generously given permission to move the instrument into their summer house. Ash herself had gotten on the phone the evening after it was delivered.

"The price for rearranging my crummy furniture is a fabulous concert when I finally get there," Marsha said to Ashley. "Enjoy yourself, honeybunch."

"Maybe I'll take some piano lessons again," whispered Ashley. "I'm thinking about it. But only here in your house."

A few minutes later, Marsha brushed aside Kristin's thanks. "What else are friends for? Whatever you need…it's yours. We will *not* let Ashley down."

Her tone had been crisp and sure, reinforcing her support for the McCarthys, and Kristin understood what was left unspoken. Her dear friend was a mother, too, with a daughter of her own.

Unfortunately, Marsha hadn't let the conversation drop at that point.

"So, tell me about this guy who went to a lot of trouble to get you the piano." Her voice held an unasked question, and once again Kristin clearly understood what her friend didn't say out loud.

"He's your neighbor—a cop, who says his career is over."

Marsha's low whistle spoke volumes. "Are you talking about Rick Cooper?"

"Uh-huh."

"Something bad must have happened to him. We've only owned the house for three years, so I don't know him well. He's not there a lot. But I like the family. Just be careful. You don't need any more problems, Kris. Besides, cops are not our favorite people these days. Not when they sit on their butts and do nothing."

Kristin, however, found herself wanting to be fair. "The case is wide open, Marsh. He's made calls. He's been great with Ash. His dog's fantastic—in fact, the dog got her to talk! As you said, Rick's gone to some trouble for us. He's a nice guy, but you don't have to worry about a romance. He's not for me, in that kind of way."

"Okay, so now I'm changing my mind. You just told me what a great guy he is. I believe you. And he's good-looking, too. So why not see where your relationship goes?"

Talk about not needing more problems.

"I'll count the reasons, Marsha. He doesn't have a job, he doesn't know what he wants to do, or what he'll earn, or where he'll live. He's totally footloose. A rolling stone, as they say. And that is definitely not for me. Or for Ashley. And also…"

"There's more? You gave me quite a list right then."

"Yes, I'm afraid there's more, and it's coming to me right now as we speak." Kristin paused a moment to organize her thoughts. "Why would I want to risk getting involved with a cop?" she asked slowly. "They can get killed on the job. You read about it in the papers all the time. Losing John was so hard. I was thinking about his death just the other day, and I'm not going down that path again."

Her friend was silent for a moment and then said in a conspiratorial tone, "I can understand that, Kris, but who said anything about forever? If he's been as good a friend as you say, what's wrong with a little summer romance? No strings. It might be exactly what you need to jump-start a fuller life. An adult social life."

Now it was Kristin's turn to be silent. "I—I don't know," she finally said. "I need to think about that."

"I know you like a sister, Kris. We both know

you're the marrying kind. But you're also a grown woman, a healthy woman, and being with someone you like is no dishonor to John. You're allowed to… explore, shall we say?"

"I am? Well, thanks for your permission, Mother." She gave her friend's remark a humorous spin, and was still chuckling after she hung up. A summer fling? Hardly. Kristin really was the marrying kind. She was no Kristin Columbus, ready to explore a new world with Rick.

Heat crept up her body, surprising her. So there was no question that she was attracted to him. Who wouldn't be with his good looks and kind heart? And even if she were willing to swim in uncharted waters, Ash didn't need a father figure who would disappear after a couple of months. Her insecurities could return worse than ever. Kristin shivered at the thought.

Nope. No romance. She and Rick would remain as they were. Friends. Just friends.

CHAPTER SIX

ON FRIDAY MORNING of the Memorial Day weekend, Kristin sat on the front porch, as she did every day, and watched Morningstar Lake come to life. She saw many more cars parked in driveways on Lakeside Road. The city dwellers had arrived, and the hustle and bustle of a new season was beginning.

She scanned the properties closest to her. One was still empty, but next door, between her and Rick, stood the Grossmans' Buick sedan. Ben and Sophie were a retired couple, probably in their seventies, who'd told her, as soon as they'd arrived the day before, that they had their lives all figured out.

"Florida in the winter and spring. Then Morningstar Lake in summer and fall," said Ben. "Our kids and grandkids visit us anywhere we are."

"Have rolling pin, will travel," joked his wife. "They come as long as I bake."

"My grandma can bake apple pie," Ashley piped up. "When we lived at her house, she made it a lot. She wanted me to eat pie with ice cream. She called it something fancy." The girl's brow creased in thought. "À la, à la…à la mode. Pie à la mode. That's what Grandma said."

Kristin tucked the comments away. Ash hadn't

spoken much about Kristin's parents since she'd arrived at Morningstar Lake, but she was right about the pie.

Sophie nodded in recognition. "There are two things a grandma has to be able to produce in the kitchen," she said to Ashley, her voice deadly serious. "Apple pie is one and chicken soup is the other. Those are the rules." The woman grinned.

Ash smiled back at her and said, "My other grandma doesn't bake. But she can play the piano. Grandpa, too."

"Well, isn't that something!" Sophie returned to her house with a promise of samples for everybody the next time she baked.

Today, Ashley would probably want to spend another six hours at the piano herself. But the weather promised to be gorgeous—too gorgeous to stay indoors. Having a beautiful lake at their doorstep would not go to waste. Swimming would be on their agenda. Kristin would insist.

Sipping her coffee, she saw Rick wave from the road as he and Quincy jogged toward her. Whether it was a ritual for him and the dog in the city, she didn't know, but a morning run certainly was their daily habit at the lake. She'd recognize him anywhere, even from a distance: how he tilted his head just so, how he held his body with elbows bent, how his legs pumped like pistons in a regular beat. He trotted up to her.

"Good morning, sunshine."

Blushes came too easily. "Hi…good morning."

His grin rivaled a jack-o'-lantern's.

She was afraid that her own welcoming smile matched his. She tossed a towel to him.

"You're a sweat hog."

"Which can be quickly remedied with a shower." He

rubbed his face and hung the towel around his neck, and she followed his every movement.

He reminded her of Patrick Dempsey, with a five o'clock shadow early in the morning. He'd take a shower next…. She pictured the drops of water hitting his wide shoulders, rivulets trickling through the wavy hair on his chest… *Stop!*

"Keep looking at me like that…" Rick squatted in front of her and took her hand. His grin was gone. "How about dinner with me tonight? Alone. My family is coming up today—my folks and my sister's crew. Ashley can stay at our house with them. She'll love Madison and Danny. Besides, Quincy'll be there, too."

A date. He wanted to go on a grown-up date because her hormones had encouraged him! Warmth radiated from his gray-eyed gaze. She was tempted. An evening alone with a handsome, attentive and kind man. An evening away from her problems.

"I think I'd like that," she heard herself say, "but I'm not sure. I can't promise."

His lips brushed her fingers, bestowing feathery kisses. "That's good enough."

Her hand tingled. She pressed it to her mouth as she watched him return to his own house, whistling cheerfully, his energy still high. He appealed to her in many ways, including physically. She barely recognized the kind of daydreams she'd indulged in recently. She enjoyed the man's friendship. He was fun, had opinions and was a great conversationalist. Time flew when they were together, and she appreciated his support. But her daydreams were definitely not platonic.

Under ordinary circumstances, she'd want to know him

better. And a cautionary yellow light blinked in her head. Keep the relationship simple. No romantic entanglements.

Unfortunately, she was finding it difficult to follow her own advice.

IF ASHLEY COULDN'T PLAY the piano inside, then she was taking her flute outside. She was adamant and said so as she cleared the kitchen table after lunch.

"Fine," said Kristin. "Today, we're getting fresh air and exercise. We're going swimming, walking, even fishing if you want. We can sit right on the dock and drop our lines."

"What lines?" Ashley's forehead wrinkled, but at least she was showing some interest.

"Aunt Marsha said there were poles in the basement." Loving friends became relatives after a while, in Kristin's opinion, and she'd used the courtesy title for Marsha all of Ashley's life.

Ash rushed to the basement door, opened it, then looked over her shoulder at her mom. "It's dark down there."

"Turn on the light. It's on the wall next to you."

"It's still too dark."

"Okay. I'm coming." It seemed Ash wasn't yet ready to be too adventurous.

They found the equipment and brought everything upstairs. The tackle box was locked, or at least stuck.

Ashley clapped her hands, her excitement obvious. "You know what that means, Mom?"

"We could use a paper clip?"

"Uh-uh. Worms. We're gonna dig for worms and put them on the hooks."

Not. At least, not Kristin.

Ten minutes later, they'd set up their beach chairs at the shore, in the shade of some birches. A load of paraphernalia surrounded them—drinks, books, fishing equipment, a flute, towels, sunscreen.

"It's like packing for a trip," joked Kristin.

"We're prepared, like the Boy Scouts."

"One day you'll rejoin your Girl Scout troop, Ash. I have a feeling you miss it."

Ashley reached for her flute and didn't reply. Soon the music of Elton John's "Daniel" filled the air, followed by Joseph Haydn's short pieces for flute, then bits from Prokofiev's *Peter and the Wolf.*

She could go on for hours. Was this any better than staying in the house playing the piano? Kristin sighed. Maybe later on, when Rick's niece and nephew showed up, Ashley would get involved with them.

The music gave way to a Scott Joplin piece—a rag—and suddenly the flute had company. Ash's eyes widened, but she kept on playing. This time the sax followed her, picking up the melody, providing counterpoint to her rhythm.

Kristin turned in her chair and watched Rick approach from their backyard. He inched closer but kept the music going without a lapse. They sounded wonderful together.

When the piece ended, Ashley jumped from her seat and twirled to discover her partner's identity.

"Rick! Rick! It's you." She ran to him and into his arms, as though she'd known him all her life. Quickly, he swung his instrument behind him on its strap, caught her with two hands and tossed her in the air as though she weighed nothing.

"You found me out, kiddo." His grin was contagious.

"Mom! Mom! This is so great." She dragged the man to the beach. "We could play all the time."

Sweet memories passed through Kristin's mind as she gazed at her child. *She's happy right now.* This was what happiness looked like on Ash in the past. She still had it in her.

"Ahh—one of my favorite activities," said Rick, spotting the fishing poles.

"Got any worms?" asked Ashley.

"You need to dig early in the morning, kiddo. It's too hot now. But if you and Quincy want to check out my car, there's a tackle box with lures we could use."

"Sure. C'mon, Quince." And they were off.

Suddenly, the beach seemed quiet. Very quiet.

Rick put his sax down, lowered himself into the vacated chair and shifted it closer to Kristin's.

"Your daughter's going to be fine—in the end."

"I'm beginning to believe it myself, especially when I see her with you."

He didn't like the frown that settled on her forehead. But he really liked how she looked in that blue bathing suit that matched her eyes. "Don't borrow trouble, as my mom always says."

"Oh, I've heard that before myself."

Better. She was smiling again. "I'm wondering," he said in a deadpan voice, "if you need any sunscreen on the places you can't reach. I'm volunteering for the job."

He loved how she blushed, how he could make her blush. He stroked her arm. "I'm teasing, Kris. But I have to be honest, too. You're different. You intrigue me. I don't meet many women with no hard edges."

"Maybe that's my problem. Maybe a harder edge is what I need. So, what kind of women do you usually meet?"

That was an easy question for him. "Streetwise. On the force. We all talk the same language, live the same way. There's no innocence, left, none at all."

She didn't respond immediately. He liked her for that. She cared enough to think about what she wanted to say.

"I imagine," Kris said, "that you're always looking over your shoulder, especially if you're patrolling the streets. I think that would change anyone's personality."

"True. And the job takes a toll. The divorce rate among cops is second to no other profession. And my marriage was no exception." Confession was good for the soul. And fair was fair. He knew about John McCarthy and why Kris was now a single parent.

"I'm sorry. It must have been painful."

He remembered a lot of fighting, a lot of silent periods. "It lasted four years. We drifted apart after a while. I think that having failed was more painful than the personal hurt. And that doesn't speak well of marriage, does it?"

This time, she answered quickly. "Maybe not for you, but John and I had a wonderful partnership. A wonderful marriage. I—I don't expect to find that again." She leaned toward him and stroked his cheek. "You're a good man, too. But you've got nothing to worry about with me, Rick. I'm as happily single as you are."

They were both lying. He could prove it right now. "And if another John came into your life…?"

He could practically see the glow around her. She'd

just viewed her personal heaven on earth. Not even on their best days had Theresa ever looked at him that way.

"Your husband was a lucky son of a gun."

"I was lucky, too." She rose from her chair and sat on the edge of his. "You sound...I don't know... forlorn...right now. Not your usual self." Leaning over, she put her mouth on his.

He didn't need a pity kiss. But he wanted her. This strong woman with the soft edges. Wanted her to want him, too. Nothing else mattered at the moment. He pulled her closer, hungry to taste, needing to know. Now his mouth covered hers, hard, searching. His tongue explored her lips, tongue, the recesses of her mouth.

She opened—and danced with him.

His heart took off at Mach speed and his pulse followed. He was on fire. A teenage boy had nothing on him.

From somewhere behind him, however, he heard a voice call, "Rick—we found it."

Ashley. And Quincy. His and Kris's interlude was over.

He left a trail of kisses along Kristin's jawline and headed toward her neck. She murmured a protest and tried to lock lips again.

"Ashley's here," he whispered.

"What? Where?" Kristin was totally disconcerted...and adorable. And now as pink as if she was sunburned.

"If you can stop blushing," he murmured, with his arm still around her, "and just sit quietly, she won't notice a thing."

"If we're lucky..." Kristin whispered back.

"How come you're both on that chair? It's going to break."

Kristin started to rise, and he let her go. If she thought it was better to move than to stay still, that was her call. She was the alpha wolf in her family, just as he was the alpha with Quincy.

Ashley walked closer, holding the tackle box in front of her with two hands. She placed it on the ground next to Rick's chair and straightened up.

"Ohh. He's got lipstick marks on his face. I get it. You kissed him, Mom." She whirled around to face her mother. "How come?"

Ash seemed confused, uncertain. Kris would probably feel guilty. Maybe he'd just spoiled his relationship with both of them when he'd coaxed Kristin's soft kiss to incendiary levels.

"To thank him, of course," Kris said, sounding admirably calm, "for being such a good sax player."

"Then you'd better give him another one," Ashley said without hesitation. "A big one. He's not just good. He's great!"

To Rick's surprise, Kris simply dimpled at her daughter and said, "I couldn't agree more."

HE'D COME OUT AHEAD with Ashley and her questions earlier that afternoon. He wasn't doing as well with his own sister right now.

"So, who's the woman?"

Rick glared at his older-by-only-a-year sister, who'd just finished tossing the dinner salad and was free to poke her finger into his chest.

"What, *exactly,* are you talking about?" he asked, exaggerating his words.

Cathy smirked and kept poking him. "We've all been

worried sick about you. Your phone calls are short, curt, and reveal nothing. Yet here you are, dancing in the kitchen. So, there has to be a woman. Maybe the one you mentioned earlier?"

"I am *not* dancing in the kitchen." What he'd been doing was whistling and setting the table with his niece. "And I didn't mention a woman. I talked about introducing Madison and Danny to Ashley. She's a nice kid and can use some friends." He hooked the ten-year-old around the neck. "Come on, Madison, let's get some fresh air."

The child giggled and went with him to the front door, while Cathy taunted, "I know a secret, I know a secret."

"How do you stand it?" asked Rick, allowing the door to close behind them.

Madison giggled again. "Mommy says it's her job to know everything. No one is allowed to have secrets while she's around."

"But I bet you do."

She wrinkled her nose. "Sometimes. But, man, she always figures it out."

He'd bet his last dollar his sister's nose was deep into her kids' business. She wouldn't ignore anything, from a tiny sniffle to a difficult math problem. She'd be as protective of Madison and Danny as Kristin was of Ashley.

"Mothers are like that," he said. "You'd better get used to it."

He shaded his eyes from the sun. "Where's your brother?"

They both spotted Danny at the same time, entangled in a spool of fishing line, while Quincy stood patiently by. It seemed like fishing line was the family menace this season.

"Oh, my God. What a mess." The big sister skipped toward her sibling, a lecture on her lips, while Rick shook his head, memories of him and Cathy flashing through his mind. Nothing ever changed. Madison was bossy like her mom, and Danny always came up with a good excuse for his "situations."

"I wanted to get it all ready for the morning," he explained when Rick approached. "So we could leave *way* early and not waste time. You know, leave in the dark."

"Stand still, pal," Rick said, trying to unravel the line. "You're wrapped up so well I could put you in a mailbox."

"No, you couldn't," protested the boy. "Not even the post office."

"Oh, Uncle Rick! He's only eight. He doesn't get your jokes."

"Well, he sure knew how to tie himself up," said Rick, finally freeing the boy and showing them the ball of fishing line. "We'll be ready to go tomorrow morning if you keep your mitts off it. Come on with me now. I want you both to meet someone."

Kristin answered his knock, Ashley right behind her. Kris's delighted expression when she saw the kids told its own story. Her daughter simply waited quietly…until Quincy nuzzled her. Then she leaned down and gave him her full love, as she always did.

When Ash looked up, she said, "Hi." And smiled.

"Uncle Rick's dog really likes you," said Danny.

"Quincy likes *everyone*," Madison said. "Don't you know that yet? By the way, I'm Madison." She stuck out her hand to Ashley, who shook it.

But Danny wasn't finished. "I know lots of things," he mumbled. "Like how you're always in trouble in school."

Madison glared at him. "School is boring. And mind your own business."

"You should mind yours."

Ashley looked from one to the other, then up at Rick. "Do they always fight?"

He shrugged. "I'm not sure."

"I don't like fighting." She faced Madison. "He's smaller than you, so don't pick on him. It's not right."

"He's my brother."

"So?"

"So, that's the way it works."

Ashley stared at the other girl for a moment, then shook her head. "Nope," she said. "It doesn't work like that here. Not at Morningstar Lake." She crooked her finger at Danny and the boy went to her. She whispered something in his ear that made him smile.

When Rick glanced at Kristin, her eyes were sparkling like blue diamonds in the sun. Next to him, she murmured, "I was hoping she'd join in with other children, but I had no idea she'd do it with such confidence."

"Seems to me all you girls are bossy. Is it in the female gene?"

She laughed and impulsively kissed his cheek. "I'll let that pass. I'm just too happy right now."

Twice in one day. Of her own volition. Life was good.

Danny transferred his attention from Ashley to his sister. "Now *I* have a secret."

"And so do I," Madison said slowly. "A better one." The girl's thoughtful gaze remained on her uncle and Kristin before the three of them went back home.

His proposed date with Kristin wasn't going to happen that night. Ash had resisted being left with his family. Too many strangers at once, regardless of the kids being there. Regardless of Quincy.

A Monopoly game, however, was in full swing in the Coopers' big kitchen, with Rick's parents slapping down their money to build more hotels on their properties. Rick was into utilities and railroads. Madison owned Boardwalk and Park Place, and Danny was in jail.

The boy wasn't concentrating. Not that he could do anything about the luck of the cards, but still, his mind was clearly elsewhere. For the umpteenth time he checked the clock. It was eight.

"Gotta go," he said, heading for the back porch, Quincy at his side.

"Just 'cause he's in jail…"

Rick ignored his niece for once and followed Danny. Behind him, he heard the others asking questions and leaving the game. Rick stood next to his nephew on the screened porch.

"What's going on?"

"That girl, Ashley—she said to go on the back porch at eight o'clock and listen. And I'd hear something special. Just for me."

When the beautiful melody of "Danny Boy" floated through the night, the real Danny said, "Hey, that's my song."

The flute. Ash was giving his nephew a gift. Sweet, sweet girl.

He glanced at his nephew, who'd heard the song thousands of times in his life. Tonight, the child stood quietly, with his head cocked and his expression thoughtful, as if hearing it for the first time. Perhaps this solo flute performance was as unique to him as it was to Rick.

Her rendition carried warmth, clarity and the beauty of a starry night. As always, the haunting melody had the power to move hearts, as proved by the utter silence of the listeners after the last note drifted away. A silence followed by wildly enthusiastic cheering and "bravo's." And then, as one voice, came a chorus of "Encore, encore." Rick thought that Sophie and Ben Grossman led the shouting from their own porch.

He held his breath, wondering what the sensitive girl would do now. Would she play something else?

She shocked him. Three Dog Night? "Joy to the World?" Holy cow, she'd changed the mood! Normally, he'd reach for his saxophone and join her, but not tonight. On this occasion, he was content to listen and learn more about Ashley through her music.

From the corner of his eye, however, he saw Madison quietly go into the house and return with her violin. His mom retrieved hers, and his dad, the clarinet. Rick hadn't come to play the sax by accident, and knew his family was itching to join in. He motioned for them to wait.

"That was lovely, Ashley," sang out Sophie. "What else can you play? Maybe something more like the first one, something that I know…?"

"Amazing how voices travel in the night air," whispered Cathy.

"Music, too," added Jerry, who often gave himself credit for being the only "professional listener" in the family, now that his son had begged for drum lessons.

"Sentimental Journey" had Sophie and Ben dancing as soon as they heard the opening notes. The big band number cried out for the sax, and after eight bars, Rick gave in. Instantly, the flute improvised, while Rick stayed true to the melody. Ashley's notes glided around his, her interpretation as exciting as any jazz musician's he'd ever heard. And as free. She played as though she'd been waiting for him to show up so she could let go.

His dad started singing, his mom harmonized, and as they'd done all their lives, Rick's family began creating a musical evening—this time with some help from the youngster two doors down.

One family member, however, wasn't happy. Quincy hadn't moved from his spot facing Kristin's house, his tail moving slowly through the entire concert. He'd turned toward Rick once or twice, had walked to the door, too, before resuming his position when Rick hadn't let him out.

But when "Sentimental Journey" was over, his dog barked, went to the door and whined. He ran as soon as Rick opened it.

"I'm going with Quince." Madison left.

"Me, too." Daniel followed his sister.

Rick stepped toward the door, as well.

"My oh my." Cathy rushed over and patted his shoulder. "Ashley and her mom must be special. Everyone's running over there. What has my kid brother gotten himself into?"

"Nothing he can't handle," replied Rick before joining the kids. And one kid's mother.

His niece had wasted no time. She'd already started on Joplin's "The Entertainer" on her violin when he arrived on Kristin's back porch.

But Ashley stood, flute in hand and hands on hips,

an expression of stoic resignation on her face. "Stop!" she ordered.

The violin stopped.

"First, what key are you in? Second, keep the beat. If you run wild, it won't work." She sighed. "You're only ten," she said from her eleven-year-old vantage point. "Have you ever played in a group with others?"

She spotted Rick then, and a wide smile covered her face.

"Mom and I agree. You weren't sad tonight. You're never sad when we play together."

He glanced at Kristin, who quickly stepped toward him. "'Tears in Heaven.' That's what she means. Rick, you can rip a person's heart out with your playing sometimes."

"But Uncle Rick is *never* sad," said Madison. "Are you?" Now her voice was uncertain.

"He plays in minor keys a lot, where the music sounds…mournful. I guess that's it. And music doesn't lie," replied Ashley.

"Neither do I," said Rick. He put an arm around each girl. "I'm not sad now. In fact, I'm very happy." He gave each one a kiss on the cheek, then studied Kristin. Her cheek was tempting. So tempting.

She must have read his thoughts because she stepped back and murmured, "Oh, no you don't. Enough for one day."

So, she was putting on the brakes. He couldn't blame her. She'd been crazy about her husband, and Rick was nothing at all like that good man. Rick was a mess. He hadn't solved any of his problems yet. He had no job, no direction. No nuthin'.

Kristin looked at her daughter. "Ash, why don't you

show the kids the piano? Try a duet with Madison. Go, go, go."

They went without argument, and she spoke quietly to Rick. "After I left you earlier, I went a little nuts. I realized that the home-selling season is right now. If Ash won't go home, I should put my house on the market tomorrow, or I might not get a buyer. People want to be in their new place before school starts in the fall. But maybe she *will* go home. I don't know what to do."

Kristin began to pace. "I earn a decent salary, but I'm not wealthy. If I move out before the house sells, I'll have two monthly payments. I can't carry two." Her voice rose, despite her best efforts. "And what if she won't go back to school? What will I do? I have to go to work. Oh, my God."

"Stop!" He sounded just like Ashley had with Madison, and despite her problems, Kristin smiled. "Kris, you're spinning out of control."

"Have I said anything that wasn't true?" she replied.

"Let's assume everything you've said was true. So call an agent. Put the house on the market."

She had a hard time swallowing. "If I do…that means we've failed. That Ashley won't recover."

"No! No, it doesn't. It means she's not moving forward on *your* timetable, that's all. But she *is* moving forward, Kristin. I can see the difference in the time you've been here."

"I thought so, too, but…"

"But she doesn't want to go home. She doesn't want to go to a movie theater, even with you. She doesn't want to be left alone."

Right. Right. Right.

"Sounds appropriate to me." He reached for her hand, squeezed it gently. "Would *you* return to the place you were assaulted? Would *you* want to go home after the perp threatened you? Threatened your family? After he told you that he knew where you lived? That he knew where you went to school? That if you told your mother what he did, he'd kill her?"

Kris froze. Could only stare at him. "Did she tell you? You, and not me? How do you know he said all that to her?"

"Because they *all* say it! Every one of these perps. They threaten in order to control the kids. Didn't the cops explain? I've worked so many cases…" He paused a moment before continuing. "If you think a sad song can break your heart, try a child murder. Or being the first responder to a situation like Ashley's. Not once, but again and again. Do you think I don't know? I know, Kris. I really do."

Her tears fell. Not quiet tears, like in the movies with glamorous actresses. No. Hers came with big sobs. Noisy sobs. Lots of tears. She cried on Rick, on his shirt, on his chest. She couldn't stop this time. Maybe she'd never stop. "My baby. My baby."

In his arms, she'd found a safe harbor for the moment. So comforted. So *not* alone. He understood. And his arms were strong.

"I hate him. I hate him for what he did to my little girl."

"I know, honey. I know."

She breathed.

"Look at me," he said.

She did, and saw his compassion for her.

"Kristin, do you understand that this perp may never be caught?"

"I want him…hanged from a tree. Put in the electric chair."

"Of course you do." He paused, then spoke slowly. "Now, answer my question. Do you understand that he might *never* be caught?"

Never slammed her, but she nodded, her head weighing a thousand pounds.

"Nevertheless, you and Ashley will have to go on, or the bastard will have won. Don't let him win. Don't let him ruin the rest of your lives."

Again, she nodded. "But how?"

"You're already doing it," he replied. "One day at a time. By repairing yourselves. Your lives have been interrupted. Your job is to reclaim them."

"You sound like Dr. Kaplan."

"Yeah. Right. I'm a real shrink," he said, sarcasm evident in his voice. "I couldn't even help myself."

"What…?"

"Forget it. That's a story for another day. Go find a new house while I search for a new career."

Look for a house? It was a big step. Kristin played with the thought seriously now. She tasted it. Pictured packing up. Pictured bare windows. She and John had bought the house, so excited about the purchase of their first home. She remembered going through the empty rooms after they owned it, hardly believing it was theirs. She remembered twirling round and round on the lawn. They actually had a backyard!

So many memories, but somehow moving felt okay, too. Recent events had shadowed those early memories and, in the end, a house was just bricks and mortar. Ashley's recovery was far more important. Maybe Ash needed a new place for a fresh start. Maybe they both did.

"I'm calling an agent," she said.

"Good. But now, I've got to get the kids home."

"Can I tell you something first?"

"Sure."

"You don't need a new career, Rick. You're wonderful at helping others, and that's what good cops are supposed to do. Think about it."

She led him into the living room where, for the first time, the two girls were in harmony with each other. "The Entertainer" sounded exactly right.

"Just like in the movie," whispered Kristin.

The piece ended then, and Madison announced with the authority of a queen, "She's excellent!"

Ashley rolled her eyes. "But if you fight with Danny, we won't play together again."

Kristin caught Rick's attention, then inclined her head at the boy. The expression on his face... He was the first member of the Ashley McCarthy Fan Club.

"Smart kid," Rick whispered. "Those McCarthy women...wow."

BOOM! BOOM! BOOM! Three gunshots from inside the house. Rick watched the sharpshooters enter first. He was behind them, adrenaline rushing through every artery and vein. He saw bright red splatters everywhere. On the man, the woman and...oh, God...on the little white jersey.

Moaning, Rick snapped upright in bed. He mopped his face with a pillow and waited for his heart rate to slow down. This was his first nightmare about the incident since he'd come to the lake. And it had been a doozy. In Technicolor, with sound effects—horribly real all over again.

Quincy jumped up next to him, licked his face, then lay down, one paw on Rick's leg. Oh, man, he felt no less needy than Ashley. And, as he'd suspected, in no shape for a relationship with her mother. He had nothing to offer the lioness, Kristin McCarthy. Rick was still too shattered, heart and soul.

CHAPTER SEVEN

THE NEXT MORNING'S AGENDA included grocery shopping. In the supermarket, Kris greeted some of the year-round residents she'd gotten to know. Anne Rules spotted her first.

"How's the homeschooling?" The woman had almost become a friend in the weeks they'd been visiting the library, offering assistance with reference books and lots of suggestions for fun reading, and a reminder about the girls' reading group. But Ashley was still hesitant about joining.

"We're almost finished," replied Kristin, with Ashley by her side. "She's studying for final exams now. I've been in touch with her regular school." Kristin took a breath. "We have a favor to ask you."

"Me?" The woman was clearly surprised. "Sure. Ask away."

"It's about her final exams," said Kristin. "Would you act as proctor, either at the library or at our house? You'd sign off that she'd taken the tests fair and square, under your supervision. You'd also get a small fee."

The librarian turned to Ashley with a smile. "I'd be happy to help out, Ashley. No problem."

"That's wonderful," said Kristin. "Thank you." They

left Anne after confirming a test date. The town was as friendly as Kristin could have wished for.

In the produce department, moving among the fruits and vegetables, they saw Mrs. Shilling. The woman recognized them immediately and came over.

"This is my lucky morning," she said, nodding at Kris, though her attention was really on Ash. "How are you, Ashley?"

"Fine." She stared at the floor.

Kristin was content to watch. Maybe others would have more effect on her daughter than she did at this point.

"What are you working on these days?" Mrs. Shilling was tenacious; Kris gave her credit for that.

Ash tilted her head and studied the older woman for a moment. "Do you know Beethoven's Sonata 8 in C Minor, the *Pathétique?*"

"Yes. Of course I do."

"It's difficult to play correctly."

"That's true," said Mrs. Shilling. "The skill level is high. Are you trying to learn it by yourself?"

"I'd started it before we came here."

Kris appreciated being the proverbial fly on the wall. She could learn a lot this way. She liked the teacher's manner with Ash—treating her with respect, as an equal, even though their skill levels were not the same.

"Try practicing each hand separately. In sections. Over and over until your fingers know what they're doing. When your hands cry out for each other, that's the time to put them together. Listen to your instincts, Ashley."

"I'll know?" she asked, her expression reflecting her wonder at the new idea.

"I bet you've memorized 'Für Elise.'"

Ashley nodded. "Most of it was easy, because the first four bars are repeated fifteen times and another six bars repeated four times."

"But then, there are those two interruptions that are not easy. In fact, they're difficult."

Ash nodded. "I practiced those over and over, and then—whamo! I put them together."

"And you'll do the same with the sonata."

On Ashley's face, a veil lifted. On Mrs. Shilling's face, joy shone.

A perfect match as far as Kristin was concerned. She reached into her purse. "Hang on a second, would you?" she asked the teacher.

After scribbling a name and phone number on a scrap of paper, she handed it to Mrs. Shilling. "We'll be at the lake for a while, and I'd like to work some lessons into our stay. Would you mind calling Ashley's piano teacher to talk about her progress and her next step? You might be a lifesaver here."

Her shopping cart was still empty, but some empty places inside herself had begun to fill. Maybe it really did take a village to raise a child. Morningstar Lake certainly seemed to qualify.

AN HOUR LATER, as Kristin opened the trunk of her car to unload her packages, she saw Cathy approach.

"Good timing. Let me help you." Rick's sister reached for a brown bag.

"It's not a problem. Ashley can do it."

"Haven't you learned never to refuse free labor?" She hoisted the bag and started walking to the house.

"I see where Madison gets it from," Kristin called

after her. Only after the words escaped did she worry about the insult.

She needn't have been concerned. The woman hooted and turned back to face her. "Yup. She's my girl."

And for one split second, Kristin was envious. How wonderful to live without a traumatic experience in the background. Cathy's daughter was so confident. She charged forward, unafraid. Unafraid of being wrong, unafraid of trying new things, unafraid of people. At the same time, she was also willing to cooperate. She didn't need to be the boss, at least not always, and not with her music. Ashley had the advantage there, being a year older. She'd had more study time and played flute in her middle school orchestra. Madison still attended grade school.

"Both your children are happy," said Kristin. "You're doing a great job."

"With the help of a very…shall we say 'hands-on' family," replied Cathy. "I can't take all the credit, or all the blame."

Cathy, modest? Kristin was surprised.

The woman sighed. "In my family, no one's shy about voicing their opinions. And certainly no one minds their own business." She waved her hand toward the sky for emphasis. "Heaven forbid we mind our own business! We were all worried about Rick, and I, for one, couldn't wait to get here for the weekend."

Oops! Here came the real reason for her visit to Kristin's house. She was investigating. Kristin placed her bag on the kitchen counter and reached for Cathy's. "Well, you don't have to be concerned about me, if that's what you're getting at."

"Concerned about you? Not at all. Just the opposite.

My brother seems so much calmer and happier since he's been here. I can't imagine it's due only to the fishing. He actually slept late today before taking the kids out." She threw Kristin a knowing glance.

Kristin held up her hand. "Don't say another word. I don't know what you're talking about, and maybe I shouldn't."

Cathy stared at her as though she had just sprouted another head. "He never mentioned what happened to him on the job before he packed his bags and drove up here?"

"He's an ex-cop. That's all I know and that's all I want to know—unless *he* wants to share it." And boy, did she owe him her attention if he needed it.

Ash trotted in, put a gallon of milk in the fridge and headed toward the door. "I'm going outside again. Quincy's back and I gotta say hi or he might forget me."

"No way would that happen," said Cathy. "Never, never, never. That dog's smarter than I am." She winked at Ash, and Ashley giggled. Then she left the house.

Kristin gazed through the window at the lake and saw Rick, Madison, Danny and Quincy in their boat, coming in to dock. She immediately understood what her daughter hadn't voiced. The dog's real family was here now. Ashley would be left out.

"The hordes will want lunch, so I've got to leave," said Cathy. "I came over to invite you guys to supper. We'll grill outside—very informal. I hope you can make it."

Kristin did not have a social calendar, but neither was she sure about having Rick's "hands-on" family in her personal life. Still, after Rick and the kids rushed to her house last night, it was probably too late to keep many secrets.

"What can we bring to the party?"

"Oh, goody!" Cathy was back in form. "Rick will be happy."

The two women walked outside in time to see Quincy race toward Ashley and cover her with kisses. "Ugh!" Ashley protested. "You're all wet and yucky, Quince." She stepped back.

"You would be too if you kept jumping in the lake for a swim." Rick joined them, T-shirt soaked, hair standing on end. Eyes bright. He jerked his head toward his sister. "From now on, it's either the dog or your monsters. Not both."

She punched him lightly on the arm. "Sure, sure, sure. When I see it I'll believe it. Ricky, the kids play you the way you play a fish—pulling in the line, letting it out, pulling it in until they catch you. And they always catch you." She grinned at Kristin. "A real fish might escape, but this fish doesn't have a chance with the kids. He wants to get caught."

Rick's complexion turned ruddy, or maybe it was too much sun. Kristin couldn't imagine him being embarrassed.

"Do you think we actually had a chance of catching anything in the lake?" he asked his sister. "With all that activity going on, we're lucky we didn't capsize—which was a strong possibility when Quince wanted to get back *into* the boat." He gazed thoughtfully at Ashley and slowly said, "I think he wanted to swim back for you."

Ash beamed, her delight mixed with incredulity. "Really?"

"Really," confirmed Rick. "But here's the hard part. Since he's 'yucky,' how'd you like to wash him with the hose and brush him down? You'll make him feel more comfortable."

As though he'd given her the keys to the kingdom, Ashley trailed after Rick toward his house.

Before following them, Cathy said to Kristin, "You should see your face when you look at my brother. If I were a cop, I'd say, 'We have a situation here.'"

"I'm sure you're mistaken," Kristin replied too quickly.

"Gotcha."

"All you've got from me are potato salad and dessert."

EVENINGS AT Morningstar Lake were still chilly at the end of May. In sweatshirts, jeans, socks and running shoes, Ashley and Kristin made their way to the Coopers' house. Kristin carried the potato salad, Ashley the chocolate cake. If they'd been back home, Kristin would have called the get-together a block party. Sophie and Ben were already there, as well as neighbors from three other houses. A second table was set up outside to handle all the food, and everyone had brought aluminum folding chairs.

"This is wonderful," said Cathy, her arms wide in welcome. "It's the opening weekend of summer, a terrific reason to party."

"Any reason is a good reason, according to you," responded her husband, Jerry. But he was laughing, and their easygoing camaraderie reminded Kristin of what she was missing in her life now. She and John had understood each other, too. They'd been the best of friends.

"That was a big sigh," Rick commented, taking the chocolate cake from Ashley and pointing toward the lake. "The kids and the hound are over there by the willow tree. See the piled-up cartons? I think Danny wanted to make a fort."

Ashley headed toward the tree, calling the dog's name. Quincy bounded right to her. Rick put the cake on the table and turned his attention to Kristin. "So, what's on your mind?"

But she was distracted as she watched Quincy greet her daughter. Maybe she and Ash *should* get a dog of their own, despite her reluctance to take on more responsibility.

"Rick to Kristin. Come in, Kristin." His hands were cupped like a megaphone in front of his mouth.

She patted his arm. "Sorry, I was in another world just now, considering a new purchase. A dog like Quincy."

A low whistle was his immediate response. "It's a big decision, bigger than you probably understand."

"A lot of work, huh?"

His gray eyes were somber. "Yes. Time and effort. Huge responsibility. Every dog needs to be not only housebroken, but also obedience trained. And a dog as big and powerful as our guy over there, even more so."

"So I'd need to be truly committed."

"Dogs are very trainable. They want to please. In your case, both you and Ashley would have to be involved in the training. The dog would have to follow her commands, too."

"It seems to me that Quincy bosses her!"

Rick's grin was delicious, but Kristin kept her mind on the conversation.

"Quincy's been supporting her," he said. "He knows she needs him. He's a therapy dog, remember? And besides, I've been in the background all the time. He checks with me."

"He checks with you? I thought they were merely playing together." She needed time to absorb this surprising information.

"They *are* playing. Quincy is having a great time. They're both having fun. But more important, Ash feels safe, she is safe, and Quincy has a purpose. Shepherds are a working breed—they *like* having a purpose."

"I'm going to the library. Research. Research. Research!"

"Good idea. And don't forget to include the costs—veterinarian, vaccines, food, incidentals. In the meantime, however, your Ashley *has* a dog. Right over there." He gazed at Quincy and the kids.

Kristin squeezed his arm. "You've been more than kind, Rick. Very generous. I really appreci—"

He brushed her words aside. "There was really no choice. Ash needed him. End of story."

He wouldn't look at her. But Kris knew there were always choices, always. Good or bad. Hard or easy. As though a layer of gauze had been pulled away, she began to see into the heart and soul of this cop. Wounded inside from the city streets, he could have kept to himself at the lake, minded his own business and just waved to her in passing. He didn't need to have become involved with her and Ashley at all. Now, it appeared that "getting involved" came naturally to him.

"I've got a lot to think about," she said. A lot more than he'd realize.

She spotted Cathy again. The woman seemed to be everywhere at once. "I was watching your sister and brother-in-law earlier. She's a firecracker and he's more subdued, but they mesh well. They have a nice rapport."

"I guess they took a leaf out of our folks' book. And I guess I didn't."

Something in his voice caught her attention, and she tipped her chin up to see him better. "Don't be so hard on yourself. I've heard there are always two sides to every divorce."

He was shaking his head before she'd finished speaking. "In the world I come from, there's only one side. And that's the *job*. The boys in blue are outstanding at the divorce thing. As I once mentioned, the rate's higher than in almost any other profession."

"I'm sorry."

He put the potato salad onto the overloaded table, then faced her. "Yeah. That's another reason to switch careers. Let someone else work the Crisis Team."

But somehow, he didn't sound entirely happy about that idea today. He didn't sound as sure of himself as he usually did.

"I know you'll make the right decision when you have to."

"Twelve years are enough."

Was he trying to convince her or himself? Something must have changed in the last day or two. "Why did you become a cop?"

He didn't answer. But his sister, who was making the rounds, had no trouble. "That's easy," said Cathy. "Because he wanted to help people and save the world."

"You sound like a commercial," Rick said. "Get out of here. Go have your own conversations."

"And you guys grab a plate. These burgers are juicy and perfect now."

Kristin searched for Ashley and spotted her still with

the other two children, eating and talking. She felt her smile bloom.

"Look, Rick," she said, nodding. "She's just one of the kids right now. Like she used to be. I'm so glad your family showed up."

"I'm glad, too. I guess they're providing a great distraction for all of us. At least, all of us who need one."

Little did he know the distraction he provided for her! She felt her cheeks burn at the thought, saw his eyes brighten with curiosity. She was saved from a reply, however, when a man's voice called out, "Howdy, folks." It was Sam Keaton, in uniform. He'd walked from the driveway to the back lawn, and now he was making the rounds.

"The sheriff!" she whispered. "Do you think he has some news about Ashley's case?"

"Whoa. Slow down," said Rick. He gently spun her around. "There could be a million reasons why he came over. Maybe my folks invited him. More significantly, he would have called you himself if he had new information."

"You're right. You're right. Sometimes I feel like I'm on a roller coaster, full of highs and lows."

"But you're not alone, Kris." Rick's voice was soft, soothing. "We're all with you. There's law enforcement, your friends at home, your friends up here, a certain canine and…the guy who owns him. We're all cheering for you."

His calm demeanor meant as much to her as his words. Her stress level plunged, and hope bloomed again. For a moment. But, like scratching a persistent itch, she wondered again why Sam Keaton had shown up.

UNLESS HIS SISTER or parents had issued a special invitation, the sheriff was visiting them for a reason. Rick figured it was only a matter of time before his old friend played his hand.

He watched Sam chat with each dinner guest. Getting reacquainted with long-time home owners, long-time friends. And maybe that's all he wanted to do that evening.

When darkness fell a short while later, Cathy invited everyone inside to continue the party. All the guests helped bring in the leftovers, but some of the neighbors turned down the second cup of coffee and went home, yawning contentedly.

In the kitchen, Rick kept his eye on Ashley. If the girl stayed, Kristin would stay. He shouldn't care one way or another. But despite all the silent arguments, even the noble arguments with himself, he did care.

Ash was eyeing what was left of the chocolate cake. She glanced at her mother, held up two fingers and tilted her head, a small smile playing around her mouth.

Kristin glowed. "Another piece? Go for it, sweetheart."

Ash was staying.

Still smiling, Kristin whispered to him, "Don't you think she looks better? Like she gained a few pounds?"

No. The kid was still too thin, still had the body of a child. Not a sign of adolescence. But Kris didn't want to hear that. "Maybe an ounce or two or three," he conceded, "but she seems healthy. And definitely happier than when I first saw her."

Kris beamed at him and Rick's pulse rate doubled. Everyone around them seem to disappear, and he saw only her. His sojourn at Morningside Lake was turning out to be better than he could have hoped.

He didn't kid himself, however, about Kristin's primary focus. Ashley would always come first. And that was fine with him. Their friendship wouldn't last forever. It wasn't realistic to think it would. Stuff always happened.

The sheriff interrupted his thoughts. "So now that we're mostly family here in the kitchen," said the lawman, glancing at the gathering from the doorway, "we have a problem to discuss." Sam stared at Rick. "And you're going to help solve it."

"You could give De Niro some competition," replied Rick, standing at the table, his hands locked on the back of a chair. "Get on with the show…and then we'll see."

"You won't let me down."

Rick remained silent. And not too happy. The man had manipulated the entire situation. The entire assembly, too. Rick's whole family was there, as well as Kristin and Ashley, Ben and Sophie, and even the Costellos, who lived on the other side of the Coopers and who'd arrived that day.

"I'm short staffed," began Sam. "Two days ago, my deputy, Pete, left on his honeymoon, which I had planned for. But today, three officers called in with a stomach flu that kept them retching all night, and left them useless. One went to the hospital. It's contagious, too, I might add."

Rick knew where this was going, and he shook his head. "I'm done, Sam. You know that." He had nothing to hide with this group. He'd known his neighbors for years.

"Captain Stein said I could borrow you."

Rick straightened to his full height. "You called…?"

He heard the incredulity in his own voice. His old "friend" stopped at nothing to get his own way.

"I have to protect this town. Your town, too. It seemed a common-sense solution, especially with the big parade scheduled for Monday. Frankly, I need help."

"But you don't really want me, Sheriff. You know what happened. I'm not up to it. Get someone else."

Sam replied in a soft voice, "I don't want anyone else. I'm looking at the best."

Rick's spine sagged and he snorted. "My armor's cracked, remember? I'm no good now."

"What I remember saying is that you're human. And that's the best trait of all for a lawman to retain."

Standoff. Sam leaned against the wall and studied the silent room. "The trouble with perfectionists," he mused, "is that they always think about the occasional failure instead of all the successes."

He focused on Rick again. "What about the dozens of awards and commendations you've earned? What about all the lives you *did* save? Answer that!"

"I never kept count."

No one spoke or moved. Except one young girl.

Ashley pulled on his arm. He leaned down.

She put her hands around her mouth and whispered in his ear. "Quincy wants to tell you something."

All else disappeared—the sheriff, the family, the conversation, his nightmare, even Ash's mom. Instantly, Rick slipped into his cop persona, as easily as he'd slip into a comfortable old sweater. Alert. Focused. Absorbing details. His attention was totally on Ashley.

The youngster pointed toward the front of the house, away from everyone else. Rick emitted a low whistle, and Quincy immediately sat at attention, eyes on him, waiting for his next order.

Rick motioned the dog to heel, and the three left the kitchen without another word.

IN RICK'S EXPERIENCE, most children used dolls or puppets to tell a story. But if Ashley wanted to talk through Quincy, as a number of others had, that was more than fine with him. The girl led him through the hall and onto the front porch, carefully closing the door behind them. She knelt next to the dog.

"You need to tell Rick something for me. Okay? Because I just heard that he's a policeman. And he's smart. And he likes to take care of us, even though Mom doesn't like that part.

"I think maybe his vacation should be over, so he can search for the man who…who…"

She started to sob, but caught herself and quickly wiped the tears away. Rick waited as she continued her conversation with Quincy. "The man who hurt me. Rick has to put that man in jail forever so he can't do it again. Then my stomach will feel better. Mom called somebody to sell our house, Quince, because the man knows where we live. But if Rick catches him, we could just go home. What if we don't have any place to go when Aunt Marsha comes back?"

Did the perp, in fact, know the McCarthy house? Could he reside in the community? Or was Ashley merely repeating what the guy had told her?

The child paused in her conversation with the dog and eyed Rick. Then turned back to Quincy and whispered, "I think I would remember more if he helped me."

Ash knew more. It was in her voice. In her quick glance at him from the corner of her eye. She was testing him. Sending him a message. Until now, she'd kept her own counsel, either because of the perp's threats toward her or to protect her mother. Rick had no doubt the bastard had promised to harm them both. And since that day, the girl had trusted no one. It could have been either fear or trauma, or maybe both, that had kept her silent until a few weeks ago. When she'd met his therapy dog.

"And you know what else?" Ash said to Quincy. "I saw Mom on the Internet doing research on guns. There were pictures all over the screen. But I think it would be better if Rick puts on *his* gun."

A heck of a lot better.

Ashley wrapped her arms around the dog's neck. "I love you, Quincy. You make me brave."

She started to cry then, with no holding back. Her face was buried in the dog's thick fur, her skinny torso heaving. That's when Rick had to blink back his own tears. He'd never seen this wonderful child cry before. He dropped to his knees, embraced her and kissed her forehead. But spoke to the dog.

"Quince, will you tell Ash that she's the bravest girl we know? She's absolutely number one."

He stroked her hair, then her cheek. "Can you look at me now, Ash?" he asked quietly, and the child complied. "Let's think about something so that you'll believe me. Remember the first time you saw Quincy... how scared you were?"

He waited for her nod.

"Now the two of you are tight buddies!"

A smile slowly crossed her face. She was paying attention, listening to him.

"Remember you were afraid to play the piano in the beginning? And now you're at that keyboard all the time. That's being brave. Every time you jump into activities you used to do, it's like kicking that bastard to hell."

Her eyes widened, but she nodded vigorously.

There were times when salty language seemed appropriate to him, even with sensitive youngsters. This was one of those times. And Ashley seemed to agree.

He wanted to ask her more pertinent questions, questions about the attacker, about her memories from the movie theater. But the girl had done enough work tonight. Seeking him out had been a giant step. He had to let her set the pace.

He simply asked, "Do you want Quincy to tell me anything else right now?"

She shook her head. "Not tonight," she whispered, holding the dog.

"That's fine, sweetheart. Whenever it's right for you."

She graced him with a dimpled smile, and one impression stood out from all the rest. He'd passed her test. Ashley McCarthy trusted him and was asking for help.

He couldn't let her down.

IT WAS DIFFICULT to make polite conversation when her daughter was confiding in someone else. Eventually, Kristin left the kitchen, meandered to the front hall and paced. She wasn't too surprised to find Sam Keaton joining her a minute later. Well, he might be useful.

"What do you think she's telling him, Sheriff? What's taking them so long?"

"I imagine we'll find out—sooner or later. Probably later. Not today. Not tomorrow. But someday. She's in good hands, so don't worry."

"Easy for you to say."

"Nah. It's never easy to watch people struggle." Sam waited a moment, then said, "Isn't your daughter seeing a therapist?"

"Yes. We've been going once a week."

"Do you go into the office with her? Or do you wait outside?"

She could figure out where he was heading with this line of questioning, but she didn't like being manipulated.

"My daughter's therapist has a Ph.D. in psychology and is licensed to practice. Her specialty is children. She knows what she's doing." Kristin waved toward the door. "Although Rick's been a terrific neighbor, he's not a psychologist. The situation here is not the same."

Keaton's brows reached his hairline. "There's where you're mistaken. Rick Cooper has personally witnessed and acted on more human behavior problems than any shrink in any office." He smiled and patted her on the shoulder. "Ashley's in excellent hands out there. He's the best of the best. Totally trustworthy."

"Well, I one hundred percent trust the dog…"

"Hoo-ha! You'll trust the man, too."

The front door opened, and the man in question followed Ashley and the shepherd into the house. Ashley's smile and her gay "Hi, Mom" had Kristin's hopes dancing again. She grabbed Rick's arm as Ash disappeared to find her new friends.

"What happened out there? What did she say?"

Rick's expression softened as he stood before her.

"You have a fabulous kid, my little lioness. You should be very proud of her. I know I am." He glanced aside for a moment, then directly at her again.

"I'm sorry, Kris, but in order to maintain her trust, I have to keep her confidences. What she shared stays between us." He took Kristin's hand and squeezed it. "I will admit that there was nothing unusual, nothing very specific this time, and I'm sure you'll agree that her trust is more important than your curiosity."

Curiosity? Was that what he thought? She pulled her hand away. "Ashley is my *daughter.* I am her *mother,*" she said in a hard and deliberate tone. "No one cares more about her welfare than I do. So don't talk to me as though I was fishing for gossip simply to satisfy my idle curiosity!"

Quicker than lightning, pain flashed across his face and was gone. But he continued speaking as if nothing had happened.

"I'm sorry if I insulted you. I didn't mean to. Ashley and I are building a new side of our relationship, and I can't share what she said." He sighed. "No matter what words I use right now, you're not going to like them, so what's the point? You're just going to have to trust me."

He studied his mentor for a long moment. "I'll do it. Get me a uniform, Sam, and I'll wear it tomorrow morning. Captain Stein will be happy. Hell, he'll be delirious."

If buttons could really pop from a man's shirt, they would have from Sam's. "I never had a doubt. And now I'll spread the word." He took several steps and halted. "You bringing the dog?"

"Nope. Ashley agreed to take care of him while I was on duty."

"She what?" Kristin's shock and annoyance rang clearly in the hall as the sheriff walked back to the kitchen. "Didn't you think I should be consulted about this?"

"No."

"No?" The man was unbelievably arrogant. Why had she never seen this side of him before? "What if I say I don't want the responsibility for Quincy?"

"I'm gambling you won't say that. We've all seen how Ashley's thriving with Quince. He's her conduit for feeling safe with her memories. And I know you, Kris. You won't hurt her by taking the dog away."

"Busted," she admitted, "but I would prefer to have been asked."

He nodded. "Message received."

He already sounded like a cop, and she was on the verge of a meltdown. Routines were changing again, and now she had to take responsibility for the dog. Oh, well…she'd consider it a tryout.

She rested her hand on the hall table. "Will this nightmare ever end?" she whispered.

"Absolutely. It will, Kris. One day, I promise it will end. But as I said, you'll just have to trust me."

He spoke with complete sincerity, but she couldn't believe his words now.

"I do trust you. But I don't think you trust yourself. When the sheriff told you to ignore your failures, I recognized that look on your face. I've seen it in my own mirror a million times. What happened, Rick? How do you think you've failed?"

She saw the tic at the side of his neck. The big swallow he took before replying.

"The details aren't important. It's enough that I failed, and one failure is too many. I won't fail again."

CHAPTER EIGHT

SHE'D HAD NO RIGHT to interrogate him about his past. After tossing and turning, Kristin got out of bed, threw on her cotton robe and brewed herself a cup of chamomile tea. A magazine she'd bought during the week lay on the table, and she started riffling through the pages. She saw nothing but Rick's face: his pain, his sincerity. She had to admit his intentions were good.

She didn't think he was pulling a power play. He thought he was doing the right thing by keeping the confidence of the victim. In this case, her daughter. Kristin could understand the theory and almost forgive that decision. But in the end, he hadn't promised to keep her informed in the future, either. He was monitoring Ashley's case, and Kristin had no choice but to go along with him. That didn't sit better with her than having to accept "We're working on it" from the Mayfield Police Department.

Trust me.

She wanted to, but he was so complicated. Much more complicated than John, with too many layers—life and death layers. John had had no secrets. No hidden stories. Of course, they'd met when they were very young, in a college math class. Too young to have many secrets. Instead, they'd had dreams. Dreams they'd shared, and on which they'd built a life. John was exactly who he seemed. A good man. A wonderful husband and father for all the years of their marriage.

Her heart stirred at the memories. Simpler times. Safer times. Oh, how she yearned for those simple times again.

A soft knock sounded at the kitchen door. The clock showed it was past midnight, but she wasn't afraid. She knew who it would be.

"I saw your light," Rick said as she let him in. Then he paused to stare. "Have you been crying?"

"No," she replied automatically. "At least, I've been trying not to." She pivoted toward the stove, away from him, and lit the burner. "I'll make more tea."

She felt his hands on her shoulders, gently massaging. "Kristin?" He whispered her name. "I'm sorry. Please talk to me."

The pressure of his fingers on her tight muscles—her neck, her shoulders, her arms—was as relaxing as a hot bath. Little by little, she felt more like a rag doll than an upright human. Her head lolled forward as more of her tension disappeared. "This feels wonderful…." She allowed herself to lean back against him.

"Better than tears."

"You…you caught me at a bad moment," she confessed. "I was looking backward, looking at the past, at happier times."

He turned her in his arms and drew her close. "I'm sorry, Kris." He kissed her brow. "Sometimes life just stinks."

"Yes. It sure does." She nestled against his broad

chest, her arms around his waist, and said, "I'm still mad at you for keeping Ashley's secrets."

"I know, and I'm sorry. But I know you understand why and accept it."

She heard the satisfaction in his voice and, to her surprise, it didn't bother her very much. Ashley's needs had to come first.

"I guess I have to," she said.

"Thank you for trusting me."

His lips found hers—a gentle kiss. A slow kiss. A kiss that rocked her senses. She pulled away. Took a breath.

"You're welcome," she said, "but I really don't have much choice."

"Everyone always has choices. And I choose this." He swooped down and kissed her again. Hard. Fast. Stunning.

And she responded to him. Hard, fast and stunning. Not wanting to let go.

"I hadn't planned that, Krissy, but I'm sure not sorry. Maybe we'll both be able to get some sleep now," he said a few minutes later, just before he closed the door behind him.

"Or maybe not," she said, throwing the bolt home.

Definitely not.

RICK WOKE EARLY, eager to get to the sheriff's office. Eager, but on edge. He couldn't deny the twitch of anxiety that raced through his body. The last time he was on the job… No! He wouldn't think about that now. He wasn't negotiating hostage crises in this country town.

He thought ahead. Even a short stint with Sam's office would require an orientation to the computer systems and local procedures and contacts. And security for the big parade the next day had to be planned. The entire community would probably show up for the event.

After a quick shower, he put on jeans and a long-tailed shirt, and strapped his gun to his waist. His cell rang.

"Cooper speaking."

"Stein here. Are you in uniform yet?"

No small talk today. "In about an hour."

"Good. But I want you in the city, Detective. So get to work, and then come home."

Whew! He wasn't wasting time. "With all due respect, Captain, don't count on it. I'm sending out résumés. The doc will tell you. Ask Romano." Rick wouldn't make any promise he wasn't sure he could keep. "But, uh…Captain? I need a favor."

Now the man started to laugh. "Résumés be damned. That didn't take long. Now I know you're on the job. What do you need?"

"Backup." Rick filled him in on Ashley's case. "I'm either going to get the perp or work with the family until they can live happily again without that closure."

"You're getting too involved."

"Blame Quincy. The kid lives next door. Only has a mother. You can guess what they've been through." He had to keep his emotions out of it. Objective assessment.

"I'll back you with Long Island, Cooper, if that's what you want. But keep me informed."

"Thanks."

"And, Cooper? I'm letting your team know you're wearing blues again."

Rick disconnected the call and stood quietly for a moment.

Stein didn't miss a trick. His captain planted seeds

and brought subtle pressure. *To serve and protect.* The mission felt right, deep inside him, but his nerve endings continued to sizzle. He shrugged it off. First day on the job. Everyone had a case of nerves on their first day.

He motioned Quincy to follow, and quietly slipped outside, wondering if Ashley would be awake this early.

He needn't have worried. The child was waiting on her front porch. The mist rising from the lake diffused the early sunlight, so that she was bathed in a soft glow. She rose from her chair as he approached.

"I'll take very good care of Quincy," she promised.

"And he'll do the same for you," replied Rick, putting an arm around each of the caretakers. "Like a pact between the two of you. A deal."

Her big blue eyes stared into his. "But the *three* of us are partners, aren't we?"

"Absolutely." He decided to test the waters. "I know your mom wants to be a partner, too, so that would make four."

But Ash shook her head. "She'd be too scared. More than now."

Her assessment might be true, but wasn't fair. He reminded himself that Ash was still a child. Perhaps a musical genius, but still a child whose thought process could be reduced to black-and-white with no room for gray.

"You're still scared, too, Ash. About your house, about going to school."

"But not as much. Now I have you and Quincy."

This could get dicey. "Because I'm a cop, right?"

She raised her elfin face toward him and took a moment before replying. "Yes…that's part of it."

"What's the other part?"

A Mona Lisa smile appeared. "'Tears in Heaven.' When I heard you play, I *knew* I'd like you and that you'd be my friend. Even though I didn't know it was you at the time."

He understood exactly what she meant. To her, music was truth and a vehicle for the person behind it. The song spoke to her.

"Ashley, do you understand that I might not be able to catch the man who hurt you? In fact, that I probably can't?"

She nodded vigorously. "But you'll try."

"I will. Is that good enough?"

"Oh, yes. 'Cause you and Quincy are going to take care of us, anyway."

Her expression held such certainty, he didn't want to disappoint her, yet he couldn't deceive her.

"We'll try to hang around, Ash, for as long as you need us."

She raised her thin arms and hugged him. "That will be forever."

His stomach twisted and plunged. Forever didn't work for him. It never had in the past, not with his lousy track record of a failed marriage and failed career. He waved goodbye to Ashley and the dog, vowing to work something out with the child later on. He simply could not fail with her, too.

AT HER DAUGHTER'S REQUEST, Kristin left Ashley at the lake that afternoon with Madison and Danny, under their mother's and Quincy's watchful eyes. She apologized for Ash's enthusiasm for being with the kids. She wondered, however, if this was a sign her daughter was ready to return to school.

The encouraging thought ran through her mind as she drove to the sheriff's office. She had an idea and was ready to act on it.

She didn't recognize the officer handling the front desk, and didn't see Rick or the sheriff. Probably just as well.

"I'd like to apply for a gun permit, please," she said when he motioned her forward.

The officer, about Sam's age, paused and sat back in his chair, staring at her. "Um...I thought I knew everyone in the county." He let the comment linger.

"I'm here for the summer," she replied, sitting down.

"Sorry, ma'am. You must be a legal resident of the county to apply."

The man didn't seem sorry at all, and Kristin was annoyed. "I live in Nassau County, which is part of this state. Can you get me an application from there?"

"Don't know about that.... You might have to appear in person just to get the application."

She drummed her fingers on the desktop. "So, there's no way you can get one faxed here?"

"Well, now...maybe. It takes six months, anyway, and you're going home soon..."

A familiar figure loomed behind the seated officer. "I thought I heard your voice."

Familiar? In uniform, Rick looked twice as big and *so* official.

"Quincy and Ash are with your sister."

His killer smile stole her breath. "So, you're here to visit me?"

"I'm gone," said the first cop, standing up. "She's all

yours. Her and her pistol permit." He emphasized the last words before he took off.

Her neighbor's smile disappeared immediately and his brow furrowed. Kristin needed a minute to regroup.

"Come on back here," Rick invited, leading her to the central work area—filled with desks, mailboxes, bulletin boards.

"He's right, you know," said Rick, approaching one of those desks. "It does take about six months to get the permit—if you fill out everything exactly right. You'll need four character references, four photographs, lots of notarized signatures. And you'll have to pay about three hundred bucks and demonstrate why you need a gun."

She hadn't spent enough time online to verify all this information, but he listed too many details too quickly to be making them up.

"And then you need to actually take a course in the use of—"

"Enough!" she interrupted, holding a hand up. She took a step toward him. "Why are you trying to stop me, when all I'm doing is figuring out how to help Ash feel secure enough to go home? Time is flying…"

He took her hand, led her into a private office, and simply stared at her beautiful face, now tinged with anxiety.

"You're killing me, Kris. I feel your pain, but a gun isn't the answer." He stepped closer and stroked her bare arm, the skin silky to his touch. She made no move to break away.

"Plenty of women carry small guns after they've been raped. I read about it." She spoke into his chest.

"Try some other reading. Try reading the horror

stories caused by innocent 'family' guns. Kids get curious, even smart ones like Ash."

Kristin shivered at the possibilities and moved closer to him, then felt his soft kiss on her temple.

He pounced. "Think about Ashley seeing you with a weapon. It will reinforce her theory that her mom is afraid, that you believe the perp will show up. For all we know, she might ask for a weapon of her own. *She* was the one violated. She has more right than you do—in theory."

Kristin let a second go by before she stepped back. "No one's rights supersede a mother's. Not even Ashley's."

Stalemate.

Rick spoke first into the silence. "Have I steered you wrong so far?" he asked quietly.

Fair question. "So what am I supposed to do? What if I can't sell the house and he comes back? Even if we relocate, bad things can happen. I must be able to defend myself and my daughter in the future." She broke out in a cold sweat. Her palms felt clammy. The more she thought about the perp, the more impotent she felt.

"Ash pretends we'll live here forever," she continued. "That can't be good."

"If pretending gets her through the day, then let her pretend. Whatever works. Your daughter is smart. She won't pretend indefinitely. She knew enough to ask Quincy for help last night."

Rick stared at Kristin as if to relay a secret message, and she felt hope stirring again.

"You spoke to Ash, and then you went back to work. You told Sam afterward…."

His decision to wear a uniform again was the post-script to his talk with her daughter. Maybe Ash had given him a description. Maybe she finally remembered details. Or maybe she'd never forgotten them in the first place, but was afraid to tell Kristin or the police. A lot of maybes.

Only one thing was certain. Ashley had made her choice and had chosen to confide in Rick. A new wave of hurt rolled through Kristin. She tried to swallow her pride.

"I am trusting you with my daughter," she whispered. "Please don't disappoint her—or me."

Trembling, she swiftly turned away from him. Rick draped his arms over her shoulders and pulled her gently against his chest.

"I have no doubt," he whispered in her ear, "that wise King Solomon would have given you the child when he decided between the two women who claimed him. You are the best medicine Ashley could have."

She twisted around, cupped his face in her hands and pulled him closer until his mouth touched hers. She kissed him. With warmth. With pleasure. And with joy.

"You've made me feel better—again. Thank you."

"I meant every word."

"I know."

"You're beautiful, Kris…especially when you blush."

She laughed, pulled away and headed for the door.

"One more thing," Rick called.

She reversed direction. "What's that?"

"Self-defense classes. You and Ash. The fastest way to build confidence and see progress."

Self-defense classes? Of course. Instantly excited, Kristin punched her fist in the air. "Absolutely, yes. Where do I sign up? You do have the best ideas sometimes."

The gleam in his eye was unmistakable. "Worth another kiss?"

She knew her cheeks were rosy again; she felt the heat. But this time she made it through the door with only a simple wave.

Suddenly, she was back. "One more thing." She echoed his prior statement. "I'm not assuming anything," she began, "but if a call from Long Island happens to come in, or if you happen to learn something regarding my daughter during the course of your work…I expect to be informed. And that's not negotiable."

HE WATCHED HER LEAVE, feeling he'd stepped successfully through a minefield. *Everything's negotiable.* He'd wanted to say it, but didn't. Mixing business with pleasure was never appropriate. He'd prefer to list Kristin solely in the pleasure column of his life. Despite all his doubts, he was drawn to her like iron filings to a magnet. Talking her out of the handgun had been touchy. *Stubborn woman.* Suggesting the self-defense classes had been inspired. He hoped she'd follow through.

"Hey, Cooper! We've got the rotation for the parade tomorrow. We rope off Main Street…"

Suddenly, his whole situation seemed funny. The last time he'd worked a parade, they'd roped off Fifth Avenue in Manhattan. Thanksgiving Day at the annual Macy's event involved huge floats and hundreds of thousands of spectators. Main Street, USA, would be just a bit different. What the hell was he doing here? And then he remembered. He'd screwed up.

Small as the parade was compared to the Big Apple's, he doubted Kristin and Ash would attend. Ash didn't like crowds of any size and, in this instance, he wouldn't push her to go. Correction. He wouldn't push Kristin to encourage it. Let the kid make up her own mind.

By the end of the day, he'd directed traffic for three hours, assisted a motorist with a flat tire, and observed Sam Keaton on the job. The man ran a smooth operation. He knew what he wanted and how to get it from his officers—even paperwork was submitted on time. The jokes, the coffee, the camaraderie. The attention at roll call to the hot sheets that listed the latest incidents in the region. It was all part of a well-oiled machine.

Protecting the town was a team effort, and somehow, without consciously noticing, Rick had become part of that team by the end of his shift. He was back on the streets, slipping into the role easily, as if he'd never been away from the job.

But that's crazy. As he headed home, he had to admit he didn't understand it. Three weeks ago, he'd thrown his badge at his C.O. And now he didn't break a sweat? It didn't make sense. He tried to analyze it and came up with only one difference: no hostage negotiation team here. He'd been off the hook.

For five minutes, that explanation satisfied him, until he reviewed his day. Less stress. Slower pace. Different culture. Finally, he whistled under his breath as the real explanation hit him. He'd been playing all day. *Playing at being a cop.*

Despite similar responsibilities, working in a rural sheriff's office seemed like a peaceful interlude compared with his regular assignment. Certainly, a crime was a crime regardless of location, but a twelve-person department in the country didn't strike him as real. It was so much calmer than his busy precinct, which had hundreds of officers on three shifts in a city that didn't sleep.

His mind drifted backward, and as he parked at the house, he felt uneasy. A bolt of anxiety shot through him. Suddenly, his chest tightened. *Boom! Boom! Boom!* He held on to the steering wheel, but forced his eyes to remain wide open this time. No more blood. No more tiny angels. No more memories.

Sweat covered him. His heart thudded ba-boom, ba-boom, ba-boom. He felt exhausted. Weak. These post-traumatic stress episodes were taking a toll. He couldn't ignore them anymore, the way he'd ignored his dreams. Reaching for his cell, he dialed the shrink. When he quit the force, he'd do it for the right reasons. First, however, he had to face his demons and figure out what to do about them.

He left a message—after all, it was Sunday night—and stared at the lights glowing in the windows, heard the faint sound of familiar voices. He didn't want to enter the fray of his noisy family. There was only one place he wanted to be. Only one person he wanted to be with. He exited his car and began walking toward the Goldman house. Toward Kristin.

SHE OPENED THE BACK DOOR, and her smile of welcome nearly knocked him off his feet. He wanted to hug her, kiss her and hold her until tomorrow—at least. She was so alive!

Instead, he blurted, "I lost a kid."

She paled but stepped forward, put her hand on his shoulder and tugged. "Come in. Please."

He sniffed something delicious baking in the oven,

and his stomach rumbled. Piano music drifted in from another room. Ashley, of course, playing a sonatina, Quincy probably snoozing on the rug next to her.

"You've made a home here, Kris," he said, nodding in approval. "A real home…in someone else's home." And if there was a bit of envy, of longing, in his voice, so be it.

"Thank you…I think." Worry etched her face as she put her free hand on his other shoulder. "Talk to me, Rick. What did you mean you 'lost a kid'? Today?"

"The whole thing came back to me just now, in the car. A flashback. Boom, boom, boom. The father shot them all."

"Oh, my God…how horrible." Now she was the color of chalk, but she stepped closer, embraced him. Hugged him tight. "Just horrible—for them, for you. You saw it?"

He swallowed hard. "Right afterward, after the SWAT team. I'm the negotiator on the Crisis Team, and I went in after the sharpshooters," he replied, his voice hoarse. "I'd been talking to the guy for fourteen hours."

Now she led him to a chair. "Sit." She reached into the cabinet and brought out a bottle of Merlot. "We can both use this…and this." From the fridge, she produced two types of cheese, and in a jiffy had a plate set out with crackers and grapes. She poured them each a half glass of the wine and sat down.

He watched her quick, efficient movements and stared at the table as though he'd never seen crackers and cheese before. "Your husband was a lucky man."

"I'd like to think so," she said softly, "but I was lucky, too."

"Luck…" Rick murmured. Lucky or unlucky? Was

life based on blind chance? "That woman and kid—no luck at all. Maybe another negotiator…"

"I doubt it. The man was mentally ill, Rick. He had to be. No sane person murders the people he loves, especially after so many hours of intervention."

True statement, but he'd dealt with these situations many times before and succeeded. He sipped his wine. Not even psychiatrists, however, could truly predict the behavior of any particular individual.

Kristin reached for his hand, her fingers gliding back and forth across the top. She was a toucher. Patting backs, stroking shoulders, offering hugs and kisses. He'd noticed that about her. Touching was how she connected with people. How she communicated. Now she pressed his palm and softly said his name.

"Rick…is this the reason you're here, at Morningstar Lake? You needed to get away from it?"

He brought their entwined hands to his mouth and brushed soft kisses against her fingers. "Yes." Simple answer. "I may not be able to share Ashley's secrets with you, but I wanted to share my own." If he wanted a chance with Kristin, he had to share the truth with her, the way she and her husband had done.

Her beautiful smile almost did him in. "I'm glad," she said. "Thank you so much for trusting me. It means a lot."

Unexpectedly, her eyes shone with humor and she grinned. "Aren't we quite the pair? We're both sort of homeless…"

"Out of work…"

"Trying to face some serious issues…"

"I'd say we're about evenly matched. I could also say, well matched," Rick concluded.

Now she looked startled. "Well matched? I'm not sure..."

He stood, and she followed suit. "Kristin...why don't we find out?" he whispered.

And then there was no more conversation. No more confessions. No more joking. Just two people communicating in the most basic way, the most telling way of all.

The kiss started gently but accelerated a moment after ignition. His tongue invaded her and she welcomed it. Her defenses were gone and her senses were spinning. Her skin tingled, and when she inhaled, the faint aroma of his cologne blended with the natural scent of man and started a cascade of remembrances. A delicious excitement that she'd not felt in so long. He wasn't John...but she deepened the kiss. And it felt good. It felt right.

Until the dog barked.

They jumped apart and turned toward Quincy and Ashley. The girl wore a smile as big as Morningstar Lake.

"Mom! Again. This is so cool." She pumped her arm. "Yes, yes, yes."

Totally flustered, Kris couldn't formulate a coherent sentence. Adding to her confusion was Quincy standing on his hind legs, front paws on Rick's shoulders, kissing his man as though they'd been separated for years.

"So, you like the idea, too, old buddy?" asked Rick as he played with his companion.

The dog whined.

"The only idea happening right now is dinner," said Kristin, scrambling for a save. She grabbed a couple of pot holders and opened the oven door.

"Five more minutes." She peered back at him. "You're welcome to stay, Rick."

His boyish grin was irresistible. "I'll be back as soon as I get out of uniform."

She leaned against the table after he left, overwhelmed by what she'd discovered. Not about Rick's past, but about her own present.

By immersing herself in helping Ashley, she'd totally ignored her own needs, her own relationships.

Rick's touch during the past few weeks had reminded her that there were *two* important people in her family.

CHAPTER NINE

DANNY AND MADISON showed up the next morning just as Kristin and Ashley finished clearing away the breakfast dishes.

"Mommy said you could come to the parade with us, Ashley. You and your mom." The boy glanced shyly at Kristin, then added, "We've got an SUV and everyone can fit."

Kris waited to see how Ashley would respond, and wasn't surprised to see her shake her head.

"I—I don't like parades, but thanks anyway. Have a good time. And make sure you don't get lost."

Her daughter sounded more like a worried adult than a child.

"Don't like parades?" squealed Madison, grabbing on to the first part of Ashley's sentence. "Why not? They're fun. There's music…and—"

Madison. So confident.

"And fire engines and Boy Scouts!" continued Danny. "There's Girl Scouts…"

"And soldiers…and the flag."

"And ice cream," added Madison. "There's lots of people, but everybody gets ice cream."

The siblings looked eagerly at Ash, their faces full of expectation. "So now will you come?"

Her daughter stood perfectly still, and Kris held her breath. *Come on, Ash. Don't be afraid.*

But Ash was shaking her head slowly. "No, thank you."

"Aww." Danny walked to Quincy, who gave him a lick. "Hi, boy." Then the child said, "I hafta take Quincy. He always marches in the parade with me."

"What do you mean, he marches?" Ashley asked, her surprise mixed with displeasure. "Parades aren't for dogs."

"Well, at the end, all the boys and their dogs bring up the tail. Get it? The tail? It's a joke word."

"I get it," said Ash, flashing a tiny smile. She reached for the dog's leash, clipped it on his collar and led him outside, the younger children following. Kris stood inside the screen door.

"Here, Danny. You can take him. I'll see you all later." Ash offered the leash to the boy, who slipped his fingers through the looped handle and started for the steps.

"Maybe you'll change your mind," he said, glancing over his shoulder.

"No. I'm fine." But her voice trembled.

Kristin stepped outside. Her daughter's expression revealed the true story. She yearned to go with the kids.

"I'll be with you every minute, honey," she said, standing behind Ashley and gently pressing her shoulders. "In fact, I'll get another leash and tie us together. What do you say?"

There was silence. Quick tears. Longing and indecision clearly etched on her daughter's face as she watched the children walk away.

"I'm afraid. I'm afraid." Her voice was a raspy whisper, her words were followed by a sob, and her body tensed under Kristin's hands.

Kristin took a breath. "Don't let him win, Ash. Go to the parade. We'll go together. Don't let him win."

Before Ash could respond, Quincy's barking distracted them.

The dog had stopped a short distance from the front steps, looking back toward the house. Waiting.

"He wants you to go with them," encouraged Kristin. "Me, too."

"I can't. I just can't." Ash started to cry in earnest, turned around and held on to her mom, sobbing against her.

Quincy yipped and immediately returned to the porch, herding Danny and Madison ahead of him, the leash now dragging on the ground. Once there, he made a beeline for Ashley and stood close, nuzzling her and "talking." The girl dropped to her knees and hugged him as she always did when she was upset.

Madison pulled on Kristin's hand and led her to the far end of the porch. "What's wrong with Ashley? She shouldn't cry because of a parade."

"Yeah," said Danny. "Even if she doesn't go, we'll still be her friends."

They were sweet children, with good hearts. No one had given Kristin instructions on what to say to other youngsters about Ashley. She decided to stick to the basics.

"Ashley once got lost in a crowded mall. I wasn't there. She couldn't find her friends, and she couldn't find a security guard or a policeman. She felt alone in the middle of thousands of people. And she was scared."

Danny's eyes couldn't get wider.

"Cell phone." The pragmatic Madison.

"Great idea," said Kristin. "We bought one the next day."

A tiny white lie that reassured Madison there was a way out of trouble. In reality, Ash hadn't had a chance to use her phone.

They returned to her and her four-legged friend. Ashley was smiling again, but now Kristin worried that dependency on the dog could become a problem in its own right.

"Ash, you have a job to do," she began. "If you don't want to watch the parade, you must give Quincy the freedom to go with Madison and Danny. You can't be selfish. Doesn't that handsome guy deserve to show off in front of everyone? Doesn't Danny deserve to have fun with all the other boys and their dogs?"

Madison said, "Don't be afraid, Ashley. I promise to stand next to you every minute. You won't get lost like in the mall."

Ash glanced up quickly. "*Mom!* What did…"

Danny walked closer, his normally smooth brow furrowed. "Every kid gets lost sometimes. Even me. One time, we were in Madison Square Garden. The Knicks were playing and a zillion people were there, and I had to go to the bathroom, and I couldn't find my way back. And you know what happened? A million policemen came and searched for me up and down every aisle, calling 'Dan-ny, Dan-ny,' and they wouldn't let anyone leave the building and they stopped the game, and all the Knicks players helped…."

Kristin worked hard to keep a straight face. Not so the storyteller's big sister.

"Danny's making it all up," said Madison, exasperation lacing her voice. "He always does that."

"No, I'm not! We *did* go to Madison Square Garden, and it *could* have happened," protested the boy. .

Kris glanced at Ash and wished she had a camera. Her eyes gleamed, her smile was genuine—sweet Lord, she actually appeared carefree!

"Mom, I never knew kids like these. They're cool even when they're fighting. They're not afraid of anything. I want to be like that."

"I know you do."

"And besides," Ashley said quietly, "I think you're right. Quincy isn't really my dog. He's entitled to show off with Danny." She remained silent for a moment, but Kristin sensed she had more to say.

Ash took a deep breath. "I think," she began, "I think we should all go to the parade."

KRISTIN'S JOURNAL—Monday, May 29—Memorial Day Evening

Ashley's brave choice paid off. For two hours today, she forgot her troubles. No shadows, no reluctance, lots of laughter. It was I who wanted to cry. But I didn't. And when I saw Rick's face—full of surprise and delight—and the warmth in his expression when he gave me a thumbs-up, I wanted to run into his arms and celebrate with him.

Of course, he was on duty, looking awfully handsome in that uniform. Ashley waved to him wildly and he came over for a quick visit where we stood in front of the town hall. Sharp-eyed as ever, he noticed the tote bag Ash and I shared, the strap big enough for both our arms to go through.

*"Nice save," he said. His entire family surrounded
us, his niece and nephew so protective of their friend,
until the parade captured everyone's attention.*

*The best part of the day was when Ash tied a red bow
around Quincy and sent him off with Danny to march.
She cheered louder than anyone else, her face alight, as
the boys and their dogs brought up the "tail" of the parade.
And then she asked, "Why can't girls and dogs march?"*

*I'll never forget this day. Another breakout day for
Ashley. Another day of hope...until the next situation
arises.*

*In the meantime, we'll share this with Dr. Kaplan on
our next visit.*

KRISTIN PAUSED in her writing, but her thoughts raced
on, replaying the rest of the day. Rick had joined her and
Ash for dinner, after the parade and after Rick's family
had returned to the city. The three of them sat together
around the kitchen table, the shepherd with his own
bowl on the floor. They could have posed for a snapshot
of the all-American family.

It excited her and it made her nervous; especially
because Ash blossomed in Rick's company. She joined
the conversation, voiced opinions. Laughed at his jokes.
Was she simply missing a father? Or did Rick make her
feel safe because of his profession? Or none of the
above? Maybe he was just a natural with children, like
Ashley's great-uncle from John's side of the family.
Uncle Sid always had silly jokes to tell, and puzzles for
the kids to figure out. Ashley adored him. And it seemed
she adored Rick, as well.

But the little imp! After dinner, Rick suggested a short
piano concert from their prima player. Her daughter re-

sponded by playing the most romantic music she could think of, classic and pop. From her extensive repertoire, she pulled out a true classic: Hoagy Carmichael's "Stardust." And that's when Rick invited Kristin to dance.

She'd been nervous. It had been a long time since she'd danced, and that had been with a different man. But Rick stood before her, hand extended. She clasped it, rose from the sofa and slipped into his arms. Strong, safe, caring…

"Oh my," she whispered.

His lips brushed her temple. "Yeah," he agreed.

And they began to move to the music, quickly learning each other's nuances. They soon danced with fluidity and grace, as though they'd been partners a hundred times before.

"You really move well," she said softly. "A natural."

"So are you."

She shook her head. "My husband was the natural dancer, and an excellent teacher."

She regretted the words, but Rick didn't miss a beat, literally or figuratively.

"Then I'm an extra lucky man."

Silently, they moved in unison, in tune with each other until the song faded away. Then they stood quietly, content to study each other, until Ashley piped up. "How about something fast and feel-good?"

Instantly came the music of Martha and the Vandellas' "Dancing in the Street." And they went at it with the gusto and fervor of teenagers.

It had been a great evening, and when they'd kissed good-night, Kris had been very glad she'd sent Ash to bed earlier. Their latest "feel-good" activity wasn't fast at all, but very lovely.

Kris put her journal away, more than satisfied with recent events. Rick's family would return next month when school was over, and remain for the summer. Morningstar Lake already seemed quiet without them. Ashley must have realized that, too, for she looked sad when she'd waved goodbye.

Kristin, however, had quietly celebrated. If Ash wanted to be with other kids, that was progress. Maybe she'd want to visit some of her own friends after she saw Dr. Kaplan next time. Sabrina would be the best choice. Ash's closest friend, the one who'd gone to the movies with her that day.

ALTHOUGH ASHLEY WAS a great kid, thought Rick, driving to work on Tuesday, she couldn't be left alone in the evening, not even with Quincy for company. If he was ever going to have true private time with Kris, they'd need a sitter. Sophie and Ben would have been acceptable, but they weren't available the following weekend. He mentally sifted through a variety of people in town, even considered Ms. Rules, as well as Sam and Doris Keaton. But after a moment's debate, he shook his head. Ashley didn't know them well enough and might object to everyone on that short list. She hadn't been away from Kristin since the incident.

He pulled out his cell phone and left a message for his dad. His folks might enjoy riding to his rescue with an extra weekend trip to the lake, and he felt sure Ash would have no objections. She'd enjoyed being with his entire family over the weekend. His folks might view it as a very worthy cause—their son was smiling again, at least sometimes. An image of dancing with Kristin did make him smile.

Once in the office, however, he had no time for day-dreams. Sam's deputy sheriff briefed the morning shift on the county hot sheets, APBs and other national crime information, reviewed the parade's crowd control and assigned Rick to a patrol car and his area of respon-sibility. It all seemed familiar. Rick supposed that when it came to briefings, certain similarities existed every-where. It was just another day in the life of a street cop. And it didn't feel too bad. Yet.

He was heading to the back lot to get his vehicle when the desk sergeant hailed him and waved toward a phone.

"For you. The girl's case."

He picked up the receiver. "Cooper here."

"This is Officer Joe Silva from the Mayfield office in Nassau County."

"You got something?"

"Maybe. We made a collar an hour ago. His victim was a young girl who knew how to scream real loud in the playground of the same middle school where the McCarthy girl goes."

Sounds in the office disappeared as Rick listened hard.

"Go on."

"Do we have a case? Don't know yet. Is there any connection to the McCarthy girl? I don't know that, ei-ther. Maybe we've got nuthin' except a sicko who likes little girls."

"I hear you." The downstate cop was frustrated. Without a proper identification, they couldn't charge him with Ashley's assault.

"Any chance of the McCarthy girl making an ID? We'd show her a lineup. We'd treat her with kid gloves."

"I know you would." But he also knew Ashley wasn't ready. Going to the parade had been a huge accomplishment. Viewing a lineup wasn't going to happen.

"Fax the guy's mug shot to the office here. I'll see what I can do from this end."

"Better than nuthin', I guess."

"Yeah," Rick said. "I'm afraid it's going to take some time."

"Time? Come on, Cooper. The case is cold already. I'm calling you out of courtesy to Evans and Wheeler—two pals of mine. Oh, and the mother. She's a regular caller. Even got your sheriff involved. Gotta keep him in the loop, too."

"Then good for Kristin McCarthy. I've been working with the kid, Joe. Keep working your end. One day that little Ashley McCarthy's going to fight back big-time."

A moment of silence stretched to two. "You really think so?" Silva's voice had gone soft.

"I do."

"I've got two daughters myself. These cases can stab ya right in the heart, ya know?"

"Yeah." Rick sighed. "I know."

He waited for the fax and tucked it in his pocket.

KRISTIN'S SMILE of welcome when she opened the door that evening sent his heart flying to the stratosphere. Genuine warmth. Genuine gladness.

He leaned down and kissed her with no words spoken. No words were needed.

"I'm closing my eyes," sang out Ashley. "You're getting mushy."

"Down, boy," whispered Kristin. "And I don't mean Quincy."

She had a point. Rick entered the room, tousled Ash's hair. "How're you doing today, kiddo?"

"Fine. Guess what? Mom's been on the phone a lot, and we're taking classes at the Y starting next week. Pow! Pow!" She raised her arms and struck phantom blows.

"Terrific, Ashley. That's great. Go easy on your mom, though, okay? She's perfect just the way she is."

He loved blondes. They couldn't hide their embarrassment. He watched the red splotches travel from Kristin's chest to her forehead.

"Let's see how perfect this meal is," she said, quickly checking the timer on the stove. "Rick, you're still in uniform. Want me to hold back while you change and get comfortable?"

It was as good an opening as he was going to get. He tapped his pocket and tried to lead into his subject slowly. "I actually have a little piece of business to talk about with you first. So maybe you should hold dinner for a few minutes."

All humor vanished from the kitchen. Two strained faces stared at him. "Nassau County arrested a predator early this morning in a school yard located at…" He took the folded sheet from his pocket and turned to the reverse side, where he'd made notes. He gave the location.

"That's my school!"

Kristin agreed.

He studied Ash and quickly knew he'd lost her, despite her initial outburst. She was staring at the wall, her eyes wide, the dark centers enlarging to cover most of the blue. Quincy moved to her side without being told, and Rick knelt in front of her. He had to try.

"Can you look at me, Ash?" He stroked her cheek and tapped her chin until she cooperated. "We need your help, honey, if we're ever going to get this guy."

Nothing.

"I've got a picture of the man from the school yard in my pocket," he continued. "Can you take a quick look and just nod if you recognize him?"

She stared over his shoulder. "It was dark," she whispered. "I didn't see anything. I don't remember." She spoke fast, too fast. But tears welled and dropped slowly.

The kid was lying. Her attacker had her believing every threat he'd made. Five consecutive lifetimes in jail wouldn't be enough for the monster lurking in Ashley's memory.

Rick communicated silently to Kris, indicating that she should join them. They both wrapped Ashley in their arms. "No more questions, kiddo," said Rick. "You're safe and sound."

"No more questions—ever!" replied Ashley.

"Only when you're ready," he murmured.

"Then that's never." Ashley started to bounce back after having the last word, and Rick said no more. Though his pal down in Nassau County wouldn't be happy.

KRISTIN'S CELL PHONE RANG at nine the next morning. She left Ash in the kitchen studying for her final exams, with Quincy at her feet, and stepped onto the front porch and into another sunny day.

"Kristin, this is Mary Gleason from the human resources department."

Her company. Her job. Kristin tensed up, but kept her tone bright. "Hi, Mary. Nice of you to call." *Not.*

"Just wanted to check in and see how your daughter's coming along."

She let her breath out very gradually. "She's making progress, but it's very slow. She's the tortoise, not the hare."

"Well, any progress is encouraging, but I'm sorry to hear that the pace is not faster." The woman's voice trailed away for a moment, and Kristin braced herself for whatever was coming next.

Now Mary spoke in a crisp tone. "Kristin, I'm sorry to bring disappointing news. You've got to cut your leave of absence short and get back here by July 5, not the original August 1 date we'd set for you. Your family medical leave and vacation cover you until June 30 and we'll give you the holiday weekend. But that's it."

"What? Why?" She quickly calculated. "That gives me only five more weeks with Ashley. It won't be enough. She won't even go near our house in Mayfield."

"I'm so sorry," Mary repeated. "But I'm sure you'll be happy about the reason. We've gotten two big new accounts—you're being assigned new projects."

Mary lowered her voice. "This is off the record, Kristin. The higher-ups want you. Top management. They trust your work and your ability to interact with customers. Mr. Stevenson himself stopped in here to inquire how you were doing. Don't blow this, Kristin. You're a single parent. This is an opportunity."

"I understand," she said quietly. "I'll get back to you." Kristin disconnected the call and stared blindly at the fluffy clouds dotting the bright blue sky. What kind of a choice was that? Her career or her daughter? She scrolled down her phone contacts and punched in her real estate agent's number.

"Have you finished the comparisons yet?" The sooner her house was actually listed, the better. "Are we ready to put it up for sale?"

"Well, that's up to you. The real estate market's depressed right now, and we don't expect it to bounce back for a year or two."

"Give me a dollar amount," Kristin said.

She listened with growing horror.

"But that's only a few dollars more than John and I paid eight years ago. That's crazy. And with the fees and moving expenses, I could even lose money." She shook her head in disbelief. "I'd be better off just staying put and waiting it out."

She glimpsed Ashley through the screen door. Her daughter happened to raise her head just then and wave. Kristin pasted a smile on her face and waved back, all the while wondering about her next step. The one easy decision she made was not to tell Ashley anything for as long as she could put it off.

HAVING RICK JOIN THEM for dinner had become a routine, just as him dropping Quincy off in the morning was. Although the stomach flu epidemic had passed, their neighbor was now filling a time gap between a newly retired officer and his replacement, so still working for Sam.

Rick had offered to leave Quincy with Ashley overnight, but Kristin knew he and the shepherd still started each day running several miles around the lake. Quincy needed the exercise to remain healthy, and Rick said he needed to run to clear his mind. He didn't talk any more about the incident that had sent him to Morningstar Lake in the first place, but Kris knew he kept in touch with his precinct in New York.

The evenings got longer in June, the sun's rays illuminating the landscape well past dinnertime before shadows from the nearby mountains cooled and darkened the area. If circumstances had been different, she and Ash would have been enjoying a wonderful vacation.

Instead, Ashley was studying for sixth-grade final exams while Kristin tried to figure out job and living arrangements.

"Trade places with me for a while," Rick suggested two nights later as they walked along Lakeside Road. Dinner was over. Ash and Quincy were visiting with Sophie and Ben and doing their own trading: a little music for a little apple pie.

Kristin had kept the phone calls from her office and real estate agent to herself until that evening, when she'd realized her thoughts were traveling in circles. She'd been trying not to burden Rick with more of her problems. After all, they weren't *his* problems. And yet here he was with a possible solution.

"Trading houses is extremely generous of you," Kristin said, "but I can't put you out like that."

"Why not?" he replied. "I rent a great place—the first floor of a two-family house with a big yard. My landlord won't mind. You'd have a longer commute, but not by much. And it's exactly what Ashley wants. Not only a new house, but a different neighborhood and a different school, too. She's still hiding from the perp, Kristin, and my place would be perfect."

They held hands as they often did on these strolls, their fingers lightly intertwined. Making contact had become as natural as hosting dinner, but much more exciting to Kristin.

"It's so…so extreme, I guess. So real," she said.

"Trading places is at least something to consider," Rick countered. "An option. And I'm flexible."

"Thanks," she said. "Thanks a lot. Sometimes…I just don't know what's best…."

"But you keep trying. You're an amazing woman, Kris." He stopped walking and stroked her cheek. "I really think you are." He took her in his arms and kissed her as though he were a thirsty man and she his oasis. Not just a brush of the lips or a little nibble, but with an urgency that demanded a response—a response she provided. He sighed with what she hoped was satisfaction.

Her own eagerness surprised her. She hadn't experienced that excitement in so many years. He made her feel young and carefree. Wonderful. She and Rick…

A car's horn shattered the moment and they jumped apart, like two schoolchildren up to no good. But it was more than good. It was terrific. The driver waved and made a victory sign.

"Uh-oh. We're going to be a topic," she said. "It's a small town."

"Do you care?"

"Not really. Kissing's not a criminal offense, is it?" she teased. And it felt too good to give up so quickly.

"I've got a different topic for you. A new one."

His tone caught her attention. "I'm listening."

He held up two fingers. "I've got a second interview for a job handling corporate security for a retail distributor. It's a lot of responsibility, including staffing and procedures."

"That's great, Rick. A second meeting. I hadn't known you'd gone on a first."

"Yeah. Last week." He shrugged. "I had nothing to say about it until now, but at this point, it's a real possibility."

He sounded more thoughtful than excited. "Tell me more," she urged.

"The company's strong, but I'd have to relocate—"

"Move?" She'd known this might happen almost from the beginning when she'd helped him with his résumé. But now her spirits flagged.

"Saint Louis, Missouri. The Midwest is a logical location for distribution centers. There's a lot to consider, but I still have another interview, and I'm sure there's competition."

But she was sure no other applicant would measure up to Rick. "Well, good luck. If this is what you want, then I hope you get it—even if it's in Missouri." She was his friend. She had to wish him well, despite the fifteen hundred miles making her feel ill.

AT 2:00 A.M., Kris ignited the burner under the kettle, went into the darkened living room and stared out the front window. Moonlight combined with streetlights to make the landscape look eerie. She was glad to be safe at home. Her worries seemed to attack more severely in the middle of the night. Her wee-hour pacing was becoming routine.

She turned toward the kitchen, and from the corner of her eye, saw two familiar figures come into view. Jogging. Running. Rick had to pass her house to reach his own. And yet she remained standing by the window, easily seen if he chose to glance her way.

He did. He motioned her to the side of her house, toward the back door.

She met him there and invited him into the kitchen.

"Seems neither of us can sleep," he said, looking steadily at her.

"Too much on my mind."

His gaze became soft, like a caress. "My mind is filled with you. Kissing you, holding you again." He gestured toward the outdoors. "I had to run it off."

Her breath hitched. He played no games. His voice, his intensity… The two of them lit a flame in each other, and she felt herself quiver deep inside.

"If you want me to leave, I—"

She twined her arms around his neck. "Here's your answer."

She tilted her head back, and he was there, his kisses slow, sensuous, delicious. She parted her lips and returned his advances. With her heart racing and her legs trembling, she had to lean against him. His kisses became more demanding, harder, hungry.

A hundred kisses later, and somehow, they were on the couch, their arms and legs intertwined. In his arms, she entered a wonderland that was familiar and foreign at the same time. An exploration of new visions, of new emotions. Exciting emotions.

"Easy, Krissy, easy," he murmured a while later, holding himself very still.

She could barely hear him through the roar in her ears—the sound of her own breathing. But she felt him move away, felt the cool air touch her skin.

"What?" she asked, confused.

"Are you on the pill or something?"

She jerked to a sitting position, almost slamming him in the forehead. "Oh, my God. No. What was I thinking?" She smoothed her nightgown down.

"Thinking didn't come into it," Rick said wryly.

Unexpectedly, Kristin started to giggle. "We're like a couple of teenagers—no brains and too eager." She caressed his cheek. "And having a lot of fun."

He covered her hand, brought it to his lips and kissed her palm. "Amen to that."

"Fun, but no game playing." Although their relationship would end one day soon, their respect for each other would remain strong—even in memory.

"Games are for children, Kristin. We're not children." He kissed her hand again, seemingly reluctant to let go. "My folks are coming up this weekend."

The change of topic seemed strange. "Really? That's a surprise."

"No, it isn't. I asked them to because the Grossmans aren't available."

He spoke slowly and deliberately, as if sending her a message. She waited.

"To stay with Ash in the evening while we go out on our own. We never got around to our date last time."

She'd forgotten all about that. "If she's willing to stay with them."

"Of course."

"Then it's only fair to warn you that the two times I've gone out since John died have been disasters. Awful. I might not be very good at the dating scene."

"You? Nah—the men were idiots."

"Well, *I* thought so…" She clasped her hands around Rick's neck and pulled him closer. "You do know how to plan ahead, don't you?" she asked between kisses.

"I'm no Boy Scout…."

But he was. He just didn't see it. "I like your ideas, Rick Cooper. It was very thoughtful of you and kind of your parents to come all this way. I just hope Ashley agrees without a problem." Kristin's voice trembled, and he immediately put his arms around her.

"I think she will this time."

He sounded confident. Maybe he had insight she lacked. Maybe she was too close to Ashley to see clearly. "You're a good man, Rick. And I hope you're right about my daughter."

A minute later, she stood in the open doorway watching him cross the front porch and descend the stairs. He whistled cheerfully and her heart swelled with emotion.

Dating Rick would be lovely but unnecessary. Courting her was unnecessary. If anyone had tried to predict her relationship with Rick, she would have howled with laughter and declared, "Impossible. A cop?" But somehow, Rick had turned her ideas upside down. He was a cop who cared.

But he was also a guy with nothing going for him—no security, no normalcy, no stability. A guy in crisis himself, who was still trying to figure out what he wanted to be when he grew up.

Despite all that, however, she couldn't hide the truth from herself any longer. She was falling in love with him one day at a time—and she was sure to pay a heavy price later on.

CHAPTER TEN

"BY THE END OF THIS self-defense course, every one of you is going to be a *W-I-T-C-H*."

Ashley glanced at Kristin, a puzzled look on her face. Kristin shrugged. She knew no more than her daughter did about the program. They'd filled out registration forms, paid their fees, signed papers about safety rules, and now stood in a room that could have been used for anything—a dance class, an exercise class, a karate class. Eight other students completed their group, two of whom were a mother-daughter combo just like them.

"That's right, ladies," continued Kelley, their instructor, who couldn't be taller than five foot two. "A *WITCH*. A Woman In Total Charge of Herself."

Ash was paying close attention, particularly when Kelley mentioned that a violent crime occurred every seventeen seconds, and one in three women would be a rape victim. Kristin, on the other hand, wanted to throw up.

"You must learn to be aware of your surroundings and listen to your instincts," said Kelley. "If someone invades your personal space, touches you, intimidates you, or just makes you feel downright uncomfortable, you make eye contact with that person and tell him to back off. Protect yourself."

The emphasis on safe attitudes and safety tips would be a part of each lesson, their coach told them. Then came the basics in physical training. Feet shoulder-width apart, one slightly in front of the other to maintain balance. Hands up in front to create distance. They moved from simple "keep back" gestures to a fighting stance with knees bent, one hand in a fist, while the other was ready to block blows.

Soon they learned simple blocks to deflect an attacker's punch aimed at the face. They practiced and practiced and practiced.

"Your reactions must be automatic, because a real assault happens fast. Most victims say they didn't have time to think."

Two hours after the class started, sweat trickled down Kristin's face, and her body ached.

"I wish we could stay longer," said Ashley, wiping her forehead as they walked to the car. "I'm glad we're coming back tomorrow."

"If my joints can take it…" How had she gotten so out of shape?

"Mom! We have to come back."

Kristin pulled her daughter to her. "Of course we will. And you know what? I think you were the best one in the class today."

"Really? I wasn't watching anyone else. Only the teacher."

"Good choice."

They were in lockstep as they walked to the car, arms around each other like girlfriends. "I love you, Ash."

"I love you, too, Mom."

She had the best child in the world, and that wonderful girl was trapped in a prison not of her own making.

"I'm very proud of you. Every day, you're getting stronger and braver."

"No, I'm not, Mom," her daughter whispered, latching her seat belt. "If I was brave, I'd be in school now taking my final exams instead of having Ms. Rules proctor me in the library here. If I was brave, we'd be home, and I'd be with my friends. Sabrina and I—" She cut herself off.

Stay calm. This was the first time Ashley had brought Sabrina into a conversation, and Kristin's antennae rose. "You and Sabrina went to the movies together. Remember?"

"No."

"I dropped you both off at the mall."

Silence stretched. Then Ashley said, "I don't remember that." She peered at Kristin, assessing her reaction, then gave an exaggerated sigh. "We have to face the truth, Mom. I'm not very brave. So there's no use asking me questions." She shrugged and quickly glanced away.

Her daughter was trying to distract her. Ashley had spoken her words as though she were acting in a play. Did she think if everyone agreed she wasn't brave, they'd leave her alone? Kris wished, not for the first time, that she knew what was going on in Ashley's head. She squeezed her daughter's hands and shifted in her seat to look at her.

"How would you like to invite Sabrina up here for a few days? We could pick her up after seeing Dr. Kaplan and—"

But Ash was shaking her head.

Kristin persisted. "You could swim, play duets, catch fireflies, go fishing—"

"No!" Ash held her stomach as if it ached. "She won't want to come, Mom. She won't want to be my friend anymore. Maybe no one will." Her voice ended in a whisper and Kristin gulped.

"That's not true, Ashley. Not according to her mom. Sabrina asks about you all the time."

So she was stretching the truth a little. Jo Anne had called a week ago to ask about Ashley, and said that Sabrina was mostly back to herself. The incident had left the girl very frightened. Ashley, her closest friend, had left her seat and never returned.

"Sabrina could actually use your help, Ash. She thinks you disappeared into thin air. And she's worried about you. Maybe if she just hears your voice, she'll know you're okay."

"You mean a phone call?"

"Exactly."

"Hmm…I'll think about it."

"I'm glad. Friends help each other, you know. That's the way it works." Kristin's hopes rose. She and Ashley were actually making some progress, so she kept pushing.

"Rick once told me that bad guys always scare their victims. They'll say they know where you live. But they really don't. They'll say that they'll hurt you again. That they'll hurt your mom or dad. But they can't. Is that what he said to you, Ashley?"

"Why are you asking me?" she protested. "I don't remember anything, Mom."

But Kris wasn't so sure. When Ashley had shared her experience musically, in the practice room, Kristin had been delighted that she'd found a way to tell her story.

Ash had taken her through the whole ordeal with a unique interpretation requiring no words. No details. Her playing had overflowed with feeling in every note, and by listening, Kristin had actually felt Ashley's emotions as she "told" the story. Her daughter had conveyed her feelings so well, Kristin had wanted to cry.

How could Ashley have revealed her experiences so well if she didn't remember anything except vague impressions? Kris didn't think she could. She must have other memories. Descriptions, words, actions.

"You might not *want* to remember. And that's okay, honey." She bestowed a quick kiss on Ash's cheek. "I know it's scary. But you and I, Ash, are a team, and I'll try to do what's best for you. If you need to change schools in order to feel safe, then that's what we'll do."

But instead of being reassured, Ashley started to cry.

And couldn't stop for a long, long time.

RICK'S PARENTS ARRIVED midmorning two days later, armed with brunch and wide grins.

"Have bagels, will travel," joked Larry.

"Absolutely," Barbara said, "and we'll come up next weekend, too. It's a beautiful ride."

The thing about having a family like his was that sometimes the important messages were unspoken, Rick realized. His folks would put in six hours on the road this weekend because he'd asked. They loved him and wanted to see him happy.

"Thanks," he exclaimed. "I really appreciate it."

"We're honored that Kristin trusts us."

He thought for a moment. "It's really Ashley, Mom. Kristin does nothing without Ashley's okay. You must have made a great impression on the kid when you were up here on Memorial Day."

"Must be my handsome face," said Larry.

"I'm betting it's your clarinet." Barbara seemed concerned for a moment. "Did you bring it?"

"You bet I did. I thought Ashley would enjoy a duet."

Barbara pointed at her own violin case. "And I thought she'd enjoy a trio."

Rick listened to their exchange and realized they were concerned about a child they hadn't even known existed a month ago—concerned because of him. The generations might be different, but it seemed most parents were the same. Kristin wanted for Ash exactly what his parents wanted for him: happiness. And like his parents, she'd do whatever it took to achieve it.

THAT NIGHT, Rick whistled the entire time he prepared for his date with Kris. Shower, shampoo, shave—definitely a shave—and cologne, but not too much. An olive-green sports shirt. Everyone said green brought out his eyes, and women always noticed the eyes. He pulled a comb through his hair. Okay. That was as good as he got. Dang, he was excited!

Dang? He caught himself. Must be Eugene's influence, the cop from Alabama who had fallen in love with a New Yorker and followed her home. Rick had given the marriage six months. Now it was four years and one baby later. He was glad to have been proved wrong.

His own social life had been nonexistent for a while, except for an occasional drink after work with his buddies. His erratic lifestyle left no time for planning. After all, negotiating was only part of his job. As well as carrying a regular caseload like any other detective, he was on call to work with special teams anywhere in the city. Hell, why would any sane woman want to get involved with a cop— especially one with his responsibilities?

The thought troubled him. He'd like a warm home life like his parents had, like his sister had. He just needed the right woman.

He strapped on his leg holster, his weapon nicely hidden under his black trousers, then grabbed his wallet and car keys, and headed for the front door. The plan was for him to escort the ladies back to his house, make sure Ash was comfortable with his folks, and then leave with Kristin.

"Be right back," he said to his mom as he passed the family room.

"Hang on a sec." Barbara rose from the sofa and stepped closer, inspecting. "Hmm…I have a handsome son. Especially when he smiles." She grinned.

Mothers! She made him feel seventeen.

When he saw Kris standing in her doorway, however, he was speechless. Definitely seventeen. Somehow, her everyday bangs looked extra sexy with the rest of her long blond hair arranged high on her head. Dangling earrings sparkled but were no match for the sparkle in her blue eyes. Because of him?

"You're beautiful." His first words of the evening popped out of his mouth totally uncensored.

She laughed and waved him inside. "We're just about ready."

Five minutes later, Ashley, equipped with her over-night bag, was cheerfully settling in with his parents and Quincy.

"Mr. Cooper and I are going to try playing a few duets together," the child said before Rick and Kris left. "Clarinet and flute will blend well. And then we'll try a trio with Mrs. C on the violin. And then we'll all have a killer Monopoly game. So don't worry about me, Mom. Stay out as long as you want. I've got my pj's, so I can fall asleep here if I get tired."

Ashley didn't seem tired at all, thought Rick, simply excited with easy-to-read emotions. She wanted her mom and him to have a good time. "Monopoly's a great idea, Ash. Just stay away from poker."

"Huh?"

They kept the conversation light as they waved goodbye and left the house. It wasn't until Kris was seated in his vehicle with her seat belt locked that she exhaled a long breath.

He heard her but didn't comment, just started the engine and headed away from town.

Unexpected silence filled the car. Kris leaned back, her head against the support.

"Just the two of us," she said. "It's nice."

An understatement. "Yep."

"It's the first time since March 11 that Ash and I have been apart willingly. I had to go to my office a few times when we stayed with my parents. She sat at the window until I returned, just watching the street."

"She's made great strides, Kristin, really impressive. But I'd like to suggest another first for tonight."

She glanced at him expectantly, and he hoped not to kill the evening before it had started.

"Let's try to leave Ash out of the conversation as much as possible this evening. Let's make this an adult-only night. Is that okay with you?"

He held his breath. She was a fierce mother.

"Yes! Absolutely." She paused a moment, and he realized she had more to say. "Sometimes I think about living an ordinary life again, and I wonder if that will ever happen. Maybe tonight we can simply be one man and one woman out to enjoy the evening with each other. That's all. No problems."

He reached for her hand. "Amen to that. Although I'm beginning to think that an 'ordinary' life is really very extraordinary."

"You're quite the philosopher, but I agree with you."

Kristin studied him as he drove. A gorgeous profile, excellent driving skills. More important, tonight Rick seemed very at ease with himself. "Your sojourn here is turning out well for you," she said.

"Better than I expected. Much better." His fingers pressed hers.

Just then, her stomach rumbled, and they both laughed. "Feed me," she demanded.

They were approaching a crossroad, and he stopped at the red light. "Anything you want," he said. "Any main course at all…as long as I get my appetizer."

He leaned over and covered her mouth with his. It was a gentle kiss, but it stole her breath and made her skin tingle all over.

She heard his quiet chuckle and unexpectedly joined in. "If that was the appetizer…" She left the thought unfinished, knowing he'd fill in the blank about dessert.

"I'd like you to meet some of my friends," he said, as he began driving again.

"Sure."

"Dinner and dancing at Bourbon Street New York sound good?"

A jazz club. "Are you going to play?"

"Not this time. My attention tonight is on you. Only on you. I figure the quickest way to get you in my arms is to dance with you."

"You figured right."

It took twenty minutes to reach the club, a popular attraction in the resort area, especially on a Saturday night. People were waiting to enter, but Rick had no problem. "Dinner reservations," he explained. "Many people come only for the music and a drink."

The combination of a medium rare steak, double baked potato and a glass of Cabernet was perfect. Being held in the strong arms of a man who knew how to keep time to the music transported Kristin to a world apart from the everyday.

"For this evening, I'm on vacation. A real vacation." She tipped her head back as they moved to a hot, slow, sizzling "Summertime." "Thank you, Rick. I didn't realize how much I needed this."

"Same here."

Laced with surprise, his voice caught Kristin's attention.

"In between tales of the one that got away, the shrink at the precinct talked to me about setting boundaries between the job and my personal life. I knew the theory, of course, but...I guess when the job becomes your whole life, boundaries are almost impossible. At least for me they were."

He leaned toward her, his mouth touching hers. "Right now," he whispered, "nothing seems impossible."

She pressed closer. "I'm glad."

They walked back to their table and the conversation never stopped.

"Tell me a little bit more about your job," said Rick. "What exactly do you do, and more important, do you like it?"

"I love it. I've always loved math classes best, and now I work with math every day. And my company offers lots of opportunities to move up. In fact, I was about to sit for my own licensing exams as an actuary when—" she gestured in the air "—all this happened. I work with statistics and formulas, computing risk. We like to say it's a 'risky' business." She leaned forward and whispered, "It's a math joke. Get it?"

He grinned. "Shades of our Danny boy. Yes, I get it."

"The bottom line is that I help compute the costs of premiums for life insurance policies."

He held up his hand. "I don't even want to know about the costs of premiums for cops. They must be out of sight. Thank goodness the department covers them."

"You've got a point," Kristin said, smiling. "So, let's see…I think I need to gather a few statistics right now." She used her spoon as a pen and pretended to take notes. "Age?"

"Thirty-five."

"Gender?"

"What?" He looked comical. "I'll let you answer that one."

"Okay…" She playfully studied him across the table. "Hmm…wide shoulders, buttons on the wrong side, deep voice. Male…all male."

"Glad you noticed."

She'd noticed, all right, from the first time she saw him. "Years of service?"

"Twelve."

"Medical history?"

"Perfectly healthy."

"Good."

He chuckled. "You're not supposed to editorialize during an interrogation."

"Hey, this is my questionnaire, buddy, so we play by my rules. Marital status?"

"Divorced."

"Are you sure?"

"Of course I'm sure."

"Any girlfriends hidden away?"

"No fair, no fair!" His resemblance to Danny was remarkable.

"Just answer the question, Officer."

He heaved a mock sigh. "Not a one. No girlfriends."

"Excellent response. How about references?"

"Do we count brilliant German shepherds?"

"Definitely."

They both chuckled and relaxed against their chairs, enjoying their absurdity, while their hands found each other and intertwined.

"Any other lingering thoughts, questions or comments?" asked Rick. "Or do I pass the test?"

"I'm having fun."

"Now, that's what I call a perfect answer." Rick nodded toward the dance floor. "Again?"

She didn't question her luck. Most of her married friends had to drag their husbands onto a dance floor.

After two more numbers, the band took a break, and

Rick led her behind the scenes, where he made introductions and was invited to sit in for a set.

"Not tonight, but I'll call you. I'd like to fill in if possible." He turned back to Kris for one more introduction. "Kris McCarthy, this is Mike Rio, the owner of the club. The man who loaned you the piano for Ashley."

Mike's gray hair was the only part of him that gave a hint of his age. Full of energy, he could have been anywhere between forty and seventy.

"I don't know how to ever thank you," she began.

He waved away her thanks. "Music is medicine," he said. "Better than any pill you can take."

"Hang on a minute," the trumpet player interrupted. "Did you say McCarthy?"

"Yes," Kristin replied.

"As in John McCarthy, who played with the Long Island Regional Orchestra?" The man's voice softened. "He had a little girl he always bragged about."

Unable to speak, Kristin tightened her grip on Rick's arm. "That's right," he said. "John was Kris's husband. And Ashley's their daughter."

The man came closer and extended his hand. She let go of Rick and clasped it. "We played together, first and second chair in the brass section. What a great guy. I was playing jazz in other bands at the same time, but he loved teaching those high school kids, and stuck with it. 'Music now and for a lifetime,' he always said."

"Thank you. Thank you very much," Kris said. "That was such a nice tribute. I'll tell Ashley I met you. She'll be excited."

"Better yet, bring her around some time," said Mike. "We'll let her play, too."

A SHORT WHILE LATER, they made their way to Rick's vehicle. The mood had changed after they'd chatted with the band. Kristin felt it. She sensed that Rick did, too, even though he hadn't said anything.

"It's not the way—"

"I guess it's unreason—"

She put her index finger over his lips. "It's not the way I envisioned the end of the evening. We were both blindsided by John's name. I'm sorry." She peeked up at him and saw his surprised expression in the glow of the moon and the parking lot lights.

"No need to apologize, Kris. Your husband was a good man."

"And so are you."

Then she was in his arms, being crushed against him. His mouth covered hers, his kiss filled with hunger and need…and something else. Something more important. A promise? A yearning?

"Your daughter needs both of us now. But in the end, a true relationship is between one man and one woman." His roughened voice reflected his emotions as clearly as his melodic saxophone did. His focus was only on her.

She caressed his face and saw his yearning, his want. She didn't know where their relationship would go at this point, but she wanted to find out. "As far as I'm concerned, the evening is *not* over. We're still on a minivacation."

His Adam's apple jumped as he swallowed hard. "And I'm prepared this time."

THE RIDE BACK to her house was quiet but comfortable. The dark country roads required Rick's attention, but he still managed to reach for her hand several times. She certainly had no objections. The simple act of holding hands made her feel special. Protected. Perhaps even loved?

They closed the car doors with barely a click, giggling like kids eager not to be caught.

When they finally made it into her kitchen, they burst out laughing. A second later, however, their laughter ended. And at that exact moment, shyness paid Kris a visit. She, who had become an aggressive, take-charge, pain-in-the-neck woman when she had to be, couldn't meet Rick's eyes.

"Hey, sweetheart." He stroked her cheek. "We're cool. It's okay."

"It's funny," she said. "I'm standing here, feeling… I'll admit it—I'm feeling awkward. But I know you are, too."

He stepped closer. "Krissy, you call the shots. I have no intention of messing up whatever it is we've got going here." His open gaze shone with truth, despite the vague "whatever." Fine with her.

"You're the first man I've been with since John," she said, "and yet I feel like I've known you for a long time. It's so strange…." *And so exciting.*

"If I'm your first, then you have nothing to compare me with…and that's good."

He swooped in for a kiss, and that's all it took for words to cease and rockets to fly. As for shyness—it didn't exist.

They clung to each other as she led him to her bedroom. Once there, they found their own truths while entangled in each other's arms and legs…and hearts. She tingled, she shivered. His skilled fingers found the right notes as he played her body. He made her swirl through a symphony of sensations as they rose together in a crescendo to the sound of "Krissy, Krissy…oh, *Krissy*."

And then they fell down, down, down from the crashing cymbals to a peaceful coda and then, finally, to a resonant chord. When she touched earth again, she stared at the special man next to her and said, "My, oh my, oh my. That was…very…nice."

He burst out laughing. "Only very nice?"

"I knocked you out, didn't I?" She beamed.

"To the next galaxy and back. Come here, woman." He pulled her closer, and she cuddled on his chest.

"Know what?" she whispered.

"What?"

"This woman…the one lying on top of you right now…feels alive again. At least for this moment."

She felt him stroking her hair, now hanging loosely, felt him gently massaging her neck. "So now I've become a sex therapist?" he asked.

"Absolutely!" She grinned and shifted position to see his face.

"Well, that solves it. I've started a new career, after all." His jovial expression turned serious after a moment. "It's really been four years for you, hasn't it?"

She nodded.

"You honor me, Kris. I hope I never disappoint you."

Never was a long time, but she didn't want to explore that now. She yawned and began to surf for her clothes. "We need to get Ash."

He peered at his watch. "One o'clock. She's probably sound asleep."

"Hopefully," Kristin said, pulling on her slacks. "But we're going to find out for sure."

He dressed in a minute, then when she yawned again, suggested she change into comfortable sweats. "It'll save you time later."

They entered Rick's house quietly, the lamp in the hall lighting their way. The front rooms were empty, but a note was propped on the kitchen table.

We had a good evening. Ashley's in Madison's bed. You two use the sofa and love seat. Blankets already there.

"Where's Madison's room?" asked Kristin, suddenly anxious to check on her daughter.

"I'll let the dog show you."

"Oh, hi, Quince. I never heard you." She rubbed the shepherd's neck. "Where's Ashley, boy?"

Quincy started in the opposite direction and led her to the first door in the bedroom wing. It stood half-open, and Kris could detect a blue light glowing from a low wall outlet.

Quincy entered first, then lay down on the rug next to the bed and stared up at the humans.

Ashley was breathing easily, sound asleep, a little smile at the corners of her mouth. Kristin's heart caught as it always did when she studied her child. She crouched next to the dog and hugged him.

"Thanks, Quincy. You're the best sitter she could have right now."

His acknowledgment took the form of a big lick on her cheek. Standing again, she started to leave…and caught the wistful expression on Rick's face as he took in the scene they presented. Wistful and something more. Much more.

He'd never uttered a word about his deeper feelings. Maybe he never would, which might be a good idea. Declarations would only complicate matters, and she didn't need more stress. Ashley was still her first priority.

CHAPTER ELEVEN

KRISTIN MULLED IT OVER in her mind and couldn't get any closer to the answer she wanted.

On Monday night, after she and Ashley had returned from their weekly trip to Dr. Kaplan's, they'd found a note on their door. "Got a gig. See you in the a.m."

True to his word, Rick had dropped in the next morning after his usual jog around the lake with Quincy. He'd stayed for a cup of coffee and talked about how much he'd enjoyed playing his sax with the jazz band. But he hadn't said a word about the incident. Kristin had had to hear about it from Sam.

The sheriff called her on Tuesday, probably thinking she'd encourage Rick to rejoin the force. She'd listened to the tale of two inebriated guests that Rick had subdued, Mirandized and prepared for their rides to jail the night before at the club. No damage to property.

"Mike Rio pressed charges against his own customers," Sam had said. "He runs a first-class operation and wants to set an example for other patrons. And Rick— well, our boy can't figure out why he jumped in. As he said to me, 'I was playing my sax, not working O.T. What the hell did I do that for?'"

Sam had seemed happy about the whole thing, and

Kristin understood why. The older man felt as though he was Rick's mentor in law enforcement.

Kristin, on the other hand, had a knot in her stomach. Law enforcement was dangerous work. Period. Even a sloppy drunk could grab a knife and lunge. The idea frightened her, and she was glad Rick was going after other positions. She hated the thought of him leaving New York, but moving to St. Louis certainly trumped getting killed.

She couldn't talk about her fears with Rick, because he hadn't mentioned the incident and she didn't think she should pry. But why hadn't he told her?

RICK WAS IN UNIFORM, the short-sleeved summer version, directing traffic again and amazed at how his wandering mind didn't get in the way of his work. The roads were becoming jammed. Little by little, more seasonal residents had shown up. Now, in the middle of June, he'd guess that at least three-quarters of the lake houses were occupied.

"Rick! Rick!"

He waved at Ashley, who'd leaned her head out of the car window to shout his name. She and Kris were probably going to the Y. They had only one more lesson to complete the self-defense course.

"See you later," he promised. "You can show me what you learned today. Both of you."

Kris smiled and drove on. Rick sighed. Neither he nor Kristin were happy. They hadn't been since last Saturday night, when they'd spent the wee hours tossing and turning on the couches. Finally, Kris had told him to go to his own bedroom or neither of them would sleep.

On Sunday morning, Ash had chattered nonstop, asking questions and watching them. His mom prepared a big breakfast and served it with a smile that matched. And all he wanted to do was get Kristin alone and make love again. Or talk. Or both.

He couldn't do any of that, however, so he'd told their audience about their trip to the jazz club, and Kristin had chimed in. Ashley was enthralled with their story about meeting her dad's friend. Her face lit up like sunshine, and she asked a million questions.

"It's hard to believe she's the same girl you brought to meet Quincy that first time," he'd said quietly.

"You're right." Kristin's voice was full of wonder. "Thank goodness Quincy's here. And thank goodness *you're* here," she murmured with a warm smile. "This summer wouldn't have been the same without you both. Too bad summer can't last all year."

As much as he agreed with her, they both knew a long-term relationship would never work. Kristin needed someone very trustworthy, not someone who screwed up so badly that three people died. She and Ashley needed someone they could depend on. Rick was okay only for the summer—at least part of it, before their leaves of absence were over.

He directed a group of shoppers across the street and suddenly, as though waking from a dream, he started to absorb his surroundings. The small shops, Dora's Diner, the post office, people strolling at their leisure. Small Town, USA. What the heck was he doing directing traffic in this rural burg when he should be working a roster of cases and handling crisis situations?

New York City teased—the fast pace, the constant

stimulation, the precinct house, his buddies. To his great surprise, a wave of excitement rolled through him, quickly followed by a wave of fear. He could fail again. Others could die. Certainly, he wasn't the only negotiator on Stein's team, but he had been at the top of the list.

Where he could do the most good.

A car honked, bringing him back to the present. His old job required concentration, and at the moment he couldn't even direct traffic and focus on his situation at the same time. He wondered what Doc Romano would say about that during their next phone call.

WILD SALMON DRIZZLED with a lemon-butter sauce, homemade coleslaw, steamed asparagus and basmati rice were on the dinner menu at Kristin's home that evening. Rick whistled in admiration as she set the table. Not the usual fare.

"Mom says we're celebrating," said Ashley glumly. "Why couldn't we just have pizza? This stuff is awful."

From an eleven-year-old's point of view, that made sense. "Actually, it's elegant," he replied. "I'm impressed, and your mom went to a lot of trouble."

"Not really," said Kris, offering him a cold drink. "But we are celebrating a lot of accomplishments tonight. Tell him, Ashley."

The child looked excited. "I finished my final exams today with Ms. Rules. Yay! She's going to mail the answer books to my old school, and I'll get to go to seventh grade next year."

"Confident, are we?" he teased, then glanced at Kristin. *Old school?*

She barely shrugged and Rick knew she was no closer

to a solution than she'd been the week before. In three weeks, she would go back to work, even if she and Ash had to rent one of those monthly hotel suites. The upside was that she'd be able to pay the charge. But he wondered what Ashley would do all day until school started.

A big sigh escaped the girl, and she shook her head. "I'm not very confident. The only subject I aced was math. But everything else—I don't know. The short answer questions were easy. Too easy. And the essays? Well, I filled up the booklets and could have written more. But now I'm worrying. I probably fell into a lot of traps with the short answers."

He took the pitcher of cold water and placed it on the table while Kristin retrieved the utensils. "Maybe you found it easy because your mom's a great teacher," he suggested. "That could be it."

"I'm not sure how great," Kristin said, "but I'm pretty strict." She looked at her daughter. "What do you think?"

Ash shrugged and avoided her gaze. "You're not so tough, Mom. I liked studying together. I wish we—"

One glance at Kristin's expression, and his heart twisted for her. She didn't want to hear the rest of Ashley's thought.

"Tell the truth, Ash," Rick interrupted. "Weren't you bored sometimes with no friends around? I saw how you enjoyed having Madison and Danny for company."

"Maybe sometimes, but then I'd practice the flute or piano, or read. I've read about fifteen books so far."

The child would have an answer for every objection he could bring up, because she was frightened. "A flute solo is nicer when it's part of an orchestra's repertoire. And for that, you need other players."

For a moment, just for a nanosecond, he believed Ash was going to agree with him. Her eyes brightened, her cheeks grew pink, and she seemed eager to discuss the topic. But then she shrugged.

"It doesn't matter."

But it did matter to her. Maybe an ensemble was the key to getting her out with others. He tucked the notion away.

"And what else are we celebrating?" he asked.

Now Ash did get excited. "We finished our self-defense lessons and tomorrow we get tested. I took lots of notes. Wanna see?"

"I'd rather see a demo."

"Sure!"

"If you think I'm letting this lovely dinner go cold…" began Kris, leaving the threat to their imagination. She motioned for them to sit down. "I'll probably forget everything I've learned when I have to take the test tomorrow."

"That's more reason to practice, Mom. Now *I* get to be strict."

"Way to go, Ashley. I like that," Rick said. "I'll hold Quincy back when you and your mom mess around."

"No need," said the girl, sliding a filet to her plate. "I've already trained him to stay away. I learned how from a book. It said to use rewards only, and that positive reinforcement was the best method." She leaned closer to Rick. "I think the book was right," she confided.

"You're quite resourceful, kiddo," he said. He looked at Kris and winked. "Feed me."

She stared at the laden table, then at him, and started

to laugh. Pleasure bloomed inside him as he realized she was recalling their date. It gave him hope.

An hour later, after the kitchen was cleaned up, he watched Kris and Ashley practice what they'd learned. He didn't know whether to laugh or cry. "If I were teaching the class, neither of you would graduate."

"I know, I know," said Kris. "We're fooling around too much. But in class, it's serious."

"Well, make it serious now."

She caught Ash's eye. "I think he means business, so get ready to block me." She grabbed a pillow from the sofa and came at her daughter from the side. Ashley swung her arm, deflecting her and ran. Kris tripped backward but caught herself.

"Better," he called. "Running is smart, Ash. Getting away is your first goal. Try blocking from the other side."

She did, then Kris practiced the same maneuvers.

"How about some strikes?" he asked.

"Palm heel," said Ashley. "For the soft spots. Eyes, ears, nose, throat…" She went through the motions with the heel of her hand against Kris's body, then demonstrated basic kicks to the groin and shin. "Touch, not tackle," she said, "like in little kids' football."

A smile tugged at his lips. His kiddo had actually learned something. "Do it again, Ash." He watched and liked what he saw. Students needed to practice over and over until their reactions were automatic.

Ash was ready to learn more, and he could teach her. But if they worked together now, their role-playing might trigger a flashback. He understood the risks very well. However, he'd worked with enough child victims in the past to know that role-playing therapy was often helpful. Often. Not always. He studied Ashley closely as she practiced with her mother and made his decision.

"Now, we're going to change the players and change the scenario a little," he said. "I'll be your partner, Ashley. I'm taller than your mother and it'll be good practice. Work it like you mean it. Blocks, strikes and kicks. And don't worry about hurting me. I'll protect myself, so go after me with all you've got." He jabbed her playfully on the shoulder. "I can take it."

She looked doubtful. "Are you sure? Mom says I'm the best one in the class."

Then the whole class needed help. "Absolutely sure. Here's the situation." He walked ten paces away from her before turning around. "We're on the sidewalk. I'm a mugger. I want your purse." Now he moved toward her, reached to grab an imaginary purse. "What do you do?"

She responded with action, throwing the "purse" at him…and running to the front door.

"Bravo!" called Kris as Ashley marched back into the living room. "Give up the purse and run as fast as you can."

"Exactly right," said Rick. "Now, one more time, except there's no purse." He motioned for Ashley to come toward him. "I'm going to grab you, and you fight back. Strikes and kicks."

He waited until they had almost passed each other, then he spun and held her around the waist. "Let's go," he growled.

That was all it took. "No!" she screamed. And went berserk. Her arms and legs swung out everywhere, her eyes were wide open and didn't blink.

"She's back there," Rick said. "Post-traumatic stress disorder."

"Leave me alone, leave me alone," she whispered frantically, then moaned. "It's dark in here. So dark, so dark… Please, please…I don't want…stop, stop, let me *go*…."

She was on the floor, arms tight at her sides, rolling left, then right. She kicked and cried, tears streaming. "It hurts, it hurts…Mom-my! Mommy, Mommy, *Mommy*…." She held that last syllable until his heart broke.

Kristin sank to the floor beside her and wrapped an arm around her daughter. "Mommy's right here, Ash," she cooed. "Right next to you. I've got you, sweetheart. I'm holding you. Come to me." The child crawled blindly and Kristin helped her, her soft voice murmuring nonstop words of comfort.

When Kris finally signaled that Ashley had relaxed, Rick ushered them to the couch and watched Ash creep onto her mother's lap.

"Hush, hush, sweetheart," soothed Kris. "It's all right. You're fine. Nobody's hurting you."

"Yes, yes he did! He did hurt me." She spoke into Kristin's chest. "That big man. He was tall and big. Bigger than Rick, maybe as tall as the ceiling."

Kris glanced at him, worry lines crinkling her brow.

"To Ash, he could have been," he whispered. Then in a louder voice, he asked, "And what else did you see, honey?"

She moved her head to see him and pointed to her cheek. "A tattoo. Right here. A snake. Curled up. Maybe a rattlesnake. Before he pulled his hat down. And then it got dark. I think…think he shut off the light."

Rick took a pen from his pocket and grabbed a piece of paper. "Ash, I know you'd rather just cuddle with your mom right now, but I need your help. Can you draw the tattoo or anything else you remember?" he asked, offering her the pen.

Her hand shook, but she produced a coiled snake with two fangs showing.

"What color was it?"

She took a moment. "Purple."

"Good. What else do you remember, honey?" He was kneeling on the floor in front of them, wanting to wrap them both in his arms, wanting to comfort them and make everything better. But that was a luxury he couldn't afford at the moment.

"His voice. A mean voice. Rough and low, like he had a cold or had pebbles in his throat."

"Then he did some talking…?"

"Yes," she whispered, and started to cry again. She turned away from him and thoroughly soaked Kristin's blouse. Rick found some tissues, made room for Quincy next to the couch and simply waited.

"Quincy!" Ash cried, when she finally noticed him. She leaned over to hug the dog. "I forgot about him just now."

The interaction between animal and child was really a beautiful thing to see. If circumstances had been different, Rick could have enjoyed it more.

"You needed people this time, Ash," he answered. "People you can trust. People who can take action to help you."

She thought about his statement for a moment, then nodded. "You're smart."

"You said he did some talking in that bathroom…"

Her eyes clouded, her chin trembled. "He…he had a knife. A big, big one."

When Kristin gasped and tightened her hold on her

daughter, Rick pressed his hand to her knee. "We're cool, Kris. She's okay. She's doing great."

"How do you know he had a knife?" asked Kristin. "It was dark."

Ash gazed at Rick in appeal, then slowly raised her hand and gestured across her throat. Rick swallowed hard. It was difficult to keep up protective barriers when family was involved. He heard a soft moan escape Kristin, but Ash didn't seem to notice, and lay back against her mom.

The girl was wiped out, and yet he had to push for more. "How about if I ask some questions, Ash, and you can just move your head up and down if the answer's yes, or shake it back and forth if it's no. Do you think we can do that?"

She nodded.

"Just to clarify, did the man hold the knife to your throat?"

Yes.

"Did he say he knew where you lived?"

Yes.

"Did he say he knew your mother?"

A hard yes.

"Where she works?"

"Yes," the girl replied. "And that he'd kill her if I told anybody. But I just can't…can't keep it inside anymore. All this time, I'd keep remembering stuff and it was always on my mind. But now it's exploding out of me. I don't know why. Something's happening to me."

"It sure is. You know what's changing?" asked Rick.

No.

"You're getting mad instead of scared."

A slow grin crossed her face. "I like that better."

Of course, that was only part of the answer. Since the incident, she'd been trying to protect her mother as well as herself. With her father gone, Kris was all she had. Whether it had been conscious or not, Ash had figured out how to get them away from the city, away from the man and his threats. She'd figured out how not to give too much away to the shrink in New York, and how to cope with the personal assault. But she couldn't hold it together forever. And she shouldn't. Those kinds of secrets could compromise her mental health for the rest of her life.

Silence enveloped them, a comfortable silence where everyone rested and gathered their own thoughts.

"I don't remember anything else," Ash finally said. "Just the hospital later." She wrinkled her nose.

Rick patted her hand. "You've given us a lot of new information, Ashley. I'm really proud of you. That self-defense class worked out a lot better than I expected."

"Hey, the McCarthy women are A students," said Kris, hugging her daughter.

"The McCarthy women are beautiful," said Rick as he stood up and got ready to leave. "Inside and out." He addressed Ashley next. "You want Quincy tonight?"

But the kid shook her head. "I love Quince, but I'm okay. He really belongs to you."

He heard the note of separation in both her words and tone, and felt a corner of his heart tear. If Kris and Ashley ever got their own dog, he'd help them to train it. That was something he wouldn't mess up.

KRIS CHECKED ASHLEY'S BED for the fourth time that night. Her daughter slept soundly, better than she had all summer. It was Kristin who was having a problem sleeping. She reached for the journal.

June 13

My guilt will never leave me. Ash called for me over and over again when that pervert had her, and I wasn't there for her. It may not be rational, but that's how I feel. How can I make it up to her? It's impossible. Can I turn back the clock? If only I had gone with them...or taken them ice skating instead. If only we had visited my parents that day...if only, if only. I can't change anything.

She put the pen down and reached for a tissue. She'd cried so much, thinking about all her regrets, that her nose was totally stuffed and she couldn't breathe.

Tonight was a breakthrough for Ash, but not the end of the aftermath. We'll both have to deal with this for the rest of our lives, but somehow we also have to put it behind us. Erect our own boundaries, just like Rick has to. We can't let it take over. Ash must get back to a routine that includes friends, public school, grandparents and a home of our own. I don't care anymore if we sell the house at a loss, we just need to have another home.

Maybe I need to speak to a counselor again. For Ashley's sake. For my own sake.

And Rick—his offer to trade places is still open.

She needed another tissue. Rick had become a part of their daily lives. And it felt so good. She loved greeting him at the door each evening. She loved feeling his arms around her, the touch of his lips on hers. The comfort of his company. But they were truly examples of the proverbial "ships passing in the night."

I don't know what lies ahead, but I'd better be prepared.

THE NEXT AFTERNOON, Kris, Ashley and Quincy were at the sheriff's office after the McCarthys passed their self-defense exams. Rick had called her cell phone, asking them to come in. He had spoken to his contact in Long Island, and it seemed none of the local gangs wore that tattoo. The cops there wanted Ashley to work with one of their sketch artists.

"I tried to talk them into letting us work with someone up here," said Rick.

"There are qualified artists who are on call for us," added Sam, "but we didn't want to push the idea until we'd spoken with you."

Kris had no trouble making this decision. "We should go back. That's where it happened, and those cops are *supposed* to be working the case." A thread of sarcasm entered her voice, and she waved her hand at the two officers in the room. "I'm sorry, guys. If you hadn't made phone calls…"

She studied her daughter, who had gone from casually sitting with the dog in front of her to hiding her face in his fur and holding him around the neck.

Uh-oh. Kristin tried to make her voice light. "Do you have an opinion about going back, Ashley?"

"Yes," she said, then raised her head. "I'm not going unless we all go. And that means Quincy, too. And Rick."

"Thanks for the last-minute inclusion, kiddo. I think we can work that out," he told her.

Rick was coming through for them again. He'd never failed them, not from that very first day. She studied him now, the man who lived in the back of her mind, a man she could count on in good times and bad, and understood why she loved him.

She hadn't wanted to fall in love with him at all. But how could she not love a man whose warmth, humor and kindness to Ashley and her were never-ending? A man who made her feel as special on a dance floor as when making love in a bed. Rick and Kristin weren't right for each other in the long run. They were a mismatched pair with messy lives. But her heart didn't seem to care about that.

He glanced her way just then, and in the next moment was at her side. "Keep looking at me like that and I'll clear out the room," he whispered in her ear.

She felt herself burn. Sam coughed. Ashley stared at them with interest. Then smiled.

"Pete's back from his honeymoon, so can I be taken off the rotation?" asked Rick, saving her from total incineration.

"You bet. We'll be fine here, and you do what you have to do with Miss Ashley. Call me when you get back." Then the sheriff stared directly at Rick. "And you might want to visit Captain Stein while you're there."

Sam shook Kristin's hand. "Good luck—with both of them."

"So are we all going?" asked Ashley. "Even Quincy?"

Of course we are, thought Kristin, *because Rick made it happen.*

"Yes, Ashley. We'll make it a family affair," said Rick, before making another call to her hometown.

Family affair? Kristin's heart started to thump. Did he realize what he'd said? Or was it just a figure of speech?

A minute later, Rick faced them again. "We're meeting the artist on Saturday."

"Maybe we could visit Grandma and Grandpa, too," said Ash.

"Why not?" asked Rick. "I bet they miss you."

"Let's call them tonight," said Kris. "Ashley, this time you can get on the phone and talk." It would be the first time she'd done so since they'd arrived at Morningstar Lake.

Her daughter simply said, "Okay."

And that was enough to make Kristin thankful.

She gazed at Rick. "A family affair it seems to be."

DREAMS TORTURED HER that night. Fragmented bits. Different scenes. But they were all about saving Ashley. In one vignette, she heard Ashley crying "Mommy," and she ran toward her voice but couldn't find her. In another, Kristin was trapped and fighting what seemed to be a black blanket. Someone on the other side of the cloth was fighting back. But she couldn't see.

"But the last one, a third one, was awful," she explained to Rick the next evening. They'd just returned from a walk along the lake and were in the backyard, strolling toward the screened porch. Ash had run inside ahead of them to pack her clothes, and Quincy had joined her, expecting a treat. The girl never disappointed him.

"There was a man in a ski mask—I couldn't see his face. He was trying to hurt me, and I wanted to fight back," explained Kristin. "But I couldn't remember anything—not one self-defense move—that I'd just learned in class." She sighed. "Maybe I'd be useless under real pressure. Maybe all those lessons were wasted."

"Let's see." Instantly, he ran a few steps in front of her, spun around and stepped toward her. "Give me what you've got." He grabbed her, and she kicked his shin gently.

"I'm serious, girl. Do it again." He went after her. With her right hand tight, she swiped quickly and got him in the nose with her palm. Then she ran.

He ran after her. *Hadn't she made a dent?* He grabbed her again and started wrestling with her. He had her arms. *Think, Kristin, think!* Her body was a weapon and she needed options. What could she use? Not arms. But she had feet. Knees. Forehead. Stomp on his foot. Knee to groin. She stomped him, she kneed him. He released his hold, and she ran again, glancing back over her shoulder. He was down.

"Oh, my God. What have I done?" She raced back and started to squat next to him. Suddenly, he reached out and pulled her against him, right into his arms. Into a kiss.

"Great job, Kris," he panted. "I just have to catch my breath." But he kept holding her close. And it felt perfectly natural to snuggle against his chest and remain there.

"You know what?" she whispered.

"What?"

"I took down a cop."

His deep chuckle sounded like music. "Krissy," he said, "I fell for you almost immediately."

CHAPTER TWELVE

AT SEVEN O'CLOCK on Friday evening, Rick parked the car in Kristin's parents' driveway. Ashley's phone call to her grandparents two nights before had been her first to them since she'd arrived at the lake, and had brought Kristin's mother to tears. The woman simply had to see her granddaughter and daughter, they'd been gone such a long time. Kristin's dad felt the same way.

Kristin was eager to see them, too—although it had felt strange to drive almost ten miles east of the exit for her own house.

Rick was staying for dinner, then going to his place in Bayside and coming back for her the next morning. It wasn't what Kristin wanted, but she couldn't think of a better arrangement. Ordinarily, she'd have taken all of them to her home. But Ashley's terrified expression when she'd suggested it had nixed that idea. And since Kristin hadn't confided in her mother about how close she and Rick were, it would have been awkward to ask if he could stay with them at her parents' house.

Before Kristin could get out of Rick's vehicle, her mom and dad were walking toward them. It was Ashley, nimble Ashley, who unlocked her seat belt and scrambled out of the car first. Ash who ran into two pairs of open arms.

"She's missed them more than she realized," said Kristin, watching the reunion.

"She's feeling differently," said Rick. "Her confidence is growing and her outlook is changing."

She and Rick joined her parents, Quincy at Rick's side.

"Why don't you introduce Quince?" Rick suggested to the girl.

Ashley beamed. "Quincy is my special friend. I love him."

She then showed off all the dog's obedience commands and rewarded him just as a trainer would. "He stays with me a lot," she added, "because Rick has to go to work and Quince would be lonely."

Kristin's mom stepped forward. "I'm Susan, and this is William," she said, putting her hand on her husband's arm. "We need to buy Ashley's special friend something just as special as he is. What do big dogs like?"

Kristin listened in amazement. What had happened to the frightened woman she'd left behind six weeks ago? Not to mention the woman who'd never wanted the mess of family pets when Kristin was growing up? She watched her folks and Rick interact as though they'd known each other for years. Either he was charming them—a possibility—or they were just showing the appreciation they would have felt for anyone who made their granddaughter smile.

"Dinner will be ready in a moment," said Susan. Then she focused on Quincy and worry lines appeared. "I don't have—"

"But I do, Mrs. Jones," Rick said quickly. "Quincy has his own backpack, right in the SUV."

Her mother smiled as though the sun had come out after a rain. Rick stared. "You resemble your daughter—so much!"

Kristin's dad laughed. "I think it's the other way around, young man. Come on, everyone. Into the house. And Ashley can tell us all about this lake."

The delicious dinner of Ashley's favorites included apple pie, which led to the story of Sophie and Ben Grossman. After the meal, Kris and Susan cleaned up while the others took Quincy for a walk.

"He's a lovely man, Kristin," said her mother. "And handsome, as well. I see how he's got his eye on you."

This was as big an insinuation as she was likely to make. Susan Jones did not butt in, she did not gossip, she did not offer opinions unless asked. Kristin understood the unspoken question.

"It's complicated…with Ashley and all."

"There's nothing complicated if two people love each other. As for Ashley—my dear, she adores him!" Her mom's warm smile reinforced her words. "Kristin, sweetheart, I just want you to be happy again."

An echo of recent conversations. "How can I be happy if Ashley is still…unsettled?" It was the best word she could come up with.

"But she's doing so much bet—"

Cheerful voices at the front door interrupted their conversation. Susan brushed a kiss on her daughter's cheek, retrieved a thick manila envelope from on top of the fridge and handed it to her.

"I think I picked up most of what you mentioned. Regardless, it's more than she has now."

"Thanks, Mom. Ash will appreciate it."

Susan called out an invitation for a second cup of coffee and the kitchen was packed again.

"Grandma has something for you, Ash," said Kristin.

She watched her daughter open the envelope, watched her eyes pop as sheet after sheet of her music slipped through her hands and onto the table.

"Look, everybody, it's my own copy of 'Liebe-sträume,' and my Bach Minuets, and Strauss—'The Blue Danube.'"

But almost immediately, her excitement slowly morphed into a frown. "But Grandma, how…? Did you go to our house? By yourself?" Her question ended in a squeal of dismay.

"Oh, not by myself, Ashley. With Grandpa."

Ashley glanced quickly from one grandparent to the other, her head swinging like a metronome. "No! No. You can't do that. Either of you. You can't. He might be there. He's big, and he'll hurt you…." She was on the way to hysteria.

As one, Kristin and Rick went to either side of Ashley. "Grandma is fine," Kris said quietly. "Grandpa is fine. They're not hurt. The perp is dust. Plain dust."

"Easy, Ash, easy," Rick said. He tapped her cheek. "Look at me."

She did.

"Breathe. In. Out. In. Out. With me. Like a duet. That's it. Very good. There. You're in control again."

The dark moments were fewer, but when they came, they rocked their lives.

Quincy nosed his way to his girl and kissed her. Immediately, Ashley fell on him with hugs. "Grandma, you and Grandpa can't go there anymore. Promise?"

"Okay," whispered Susan.

Her mom had aged ten years in two minutes, thought Kristin. She stepped closer to her. "I'm sorry, Mom," she murmured. "I didn't anticipate this. Ash really is doing better. Honestly." Kristin turned to her daughter. "How about showing Grandma and Grandpa our moves?"

"Hey!" exclaimed Ashley, getting up from the floor. "I've got a great idea. Grandma and Grandpa should take self-defense classes, too. Let's show them, Mom."

After ten minutes of jab, jab, block, block, Kris sent Ashley to bed and extended a hand to Rick. "Want to take a walk?"

He clasped it and they stepped outside, closing the door behind them. Then he kissed her.

"I've wanted to do that for the last hour," he said. "And this, too." His lips found hers again.

She responded to him as though it was their first time together. Exploring. Getting to know more. It was all good. Sweet. Wonderful.

"Ahh, Krissy."

"Yeah, I know," she whispered. "And thanks for how you helped in there."

"You're welcome. But what I said at the lake is still true. This is about you and me." And he kissed her again.

A discreet cough made them jump apart. Susan stood in the doorway.

"William and I were just saying how silly it is for you to drive all the way to Bayside and then back in the morning before you go to the police station. Please stay here with us tonight, Rick. You and your wonderful dog."

"She took the words right out of my mouth," Kris

whispered under her breath. She was rewarded with another kiss.

"It would have taken only an hour each way," he said, "but I accept."

HE'D NEVER BEEN to this Nassau County precinct, but he could have found his way around the redbrick building in five minutes. Kristin's arm was around her daughter— they walked in tandem—and Rick figured he was definitely the most relaxed member of his little party.

They'd left the Joneses' house in high enough spirits— even had some breakfast—but as they'd approached their destination, the ladies had become quieter. And now, he could sense Kristin's nerve endings vibrating. Whether Ash was nervous herself, or whether she'd picked up on her mother's feelings, he didn't know. But her complexion seemed paler than usual and she held on to the shepherd's leash so tightly her fingertips showed white. Her death grip was unnecessary. Quincy, always sensitive to her needs, made no move to be anywhere else.

"We're here to see Detective Silva, that's Joe Silva," said Rick, putting his badge on the reception desk.

"The dog's working?"

"Check the collar." He'd put Quincy's therapy-dog badge on earlier.

"Okay, I got it. You're here to work with Sandy Page. Have a seat. I'll be right back."

Ashley sat on a wooden bench; Quincy lay on the floor at her feet. Kristin paced. Five steps left, five steps right. Her mouth was pressed into a line. She glanced at her watch, at the ceiling, at the wall posters. Everywhere but at Rick.

His muscles tightened as he watched her. She hated the place. She distrusted cops. So much laughter and loving had passed between them, he'd thought that attitude was a thing of the past.

She stepped close to him. "Don't you think they should have found him by now? Maybe they never tried until you and your friends called. And that was really too late. Even the advocate assigned to us didn't get more information than I already had."

Rick took her hand, caressed her fingers, and felt her squeeze back. "It's because they didn't have any *new* information. But you know the case is still open, Kristin. Someone is assigned to it, and now Ashley has more to contribute."

"Ashley! Somehow that doesn't seem fair. Ash is the victim here. Does she also have to *solve* the crime?"

Well, yes. Victims did have stories to tell, even victims of cold cases years old. But he didn't need another display of protective parenting. More important, Ashley didn't need it. He chose to come down hard.

"Keep your cool, Kristin, or you'll upset whatever balance Ashley's found inside herself since last night. It seems to me she's doing a lot better than you." At this point, he was quite certain his words were true.

A petite brunette with a friendly smile came out to the waiting room just then, waved to Rick and Kristin, but zeroed in on Ash.

"Hi, Ashley. I'm Sandy. And that has got to be the most gorgeous dog I've ever seen in my whole life." She knelt down to greet the shepherd and rubbed him under the chin. Quincy accepted the attention with a yawn and a lick.

"Oh, he's a love, isn't he?"

"And he's smart," Ashley said. "Very, very smart. Wanna hear a joke?" She addressed the dog. "What's on the top of the building, Quince?"

"Woof."

To her credit, Sandy laughed as though her funny bone was being jostled. Then she extended her hand.

"Come on, Ashley. Maybe you and your handsome date here can help me draw some pictures."

"I can draw…."

"Great! I've got zillions of pencils and crayons you can use with me."

And without a backward glance, they were gone through the connecting door.

Kristin stood frozen in place, but Rick's chest swelled with pride at the artist's people skills.

"And that, sweetheart, is police work at its best."

"Is she a cop?"

"Maybe. Or she may be an independent contract artist trained in forensics."

Kristin frowned in confusion. "But you can't train a personality, can you? And hers…? Why, Ashley went right off with her…." She turned her head and stared again at the closed door.

"And that means we might have a fair shot at getting an excellent rendition of the perp. Sandy knows what she's doing."

"It seems everyone knows what they're doing… except me." Kris's voice quivered and he took her in his arms, uncaring of who else was in the room.

"Krissy, Krissy. Your job is the hardest. No one else is the mother. You're doing fine. Great. You're fabulous."

She leaned against his chest, seemingly content to rest there indefinitely. He had no objections.

"I have to keep my wits about me," she whispered. "Like you said, I have to keep my cool."

He wanted to hold her forever. This woman who tried so hard to do the right things. This fighter who managed to bounce back every time she fell down. This lover who could twist his heart without even realizing it. He swallowed a chuckle at the irony. Cops weren't supposed to have a heart, were they? He was definitely in the wrong profession.

She was proud of her calm frame of mind when Joe Silva invited them inside. In his forties, alert, and with an air of confidence, Detective Silva started by offering them a cup of the station's best sludge, and making a few innocuous remarks. Rick and he exchanged work information, and Kristin enjoyed watching the two men size each other up. It was so obvious and such a male thing, she actually turned away to hide a smile.

When Joe asked about Ashley, he focused his attention on Kristin. Totally on Kristin. His interest was matched by his concern.

"I'm a father," he said. "I know where you're coming from. We're in this together, Mrs. McCarthy, and I feel your frustration." He started counting on his fingers. "No DNA match in the system. No witnesses. We really had nothing."

He seemed to have more to say, so she sat forward in her chair and waited.

"We rounded up all the registered sex offenders in the area, even without the match. If they had friends visiting, we brought them in, too. We sent a description of the incident throughout the country, and here in the metro area, we told all departments to double their surveillance around malls and theater complexes. We contacted theater managers about their security. We certainly combed our own streets that day and for days and nights afterward."

He switched his attention to Rick. "The case was on the hot sheets every day for weeks."

Then the officer swallowed some coffee and said softly, "There's not a cop in this place who doesn't want to make the collar, Mrs. McCarthy. Not a one. We haven't forgotten about your daughter."

Her eyes filled, and for the very first time, Kristin believed.

"Thank you. Thank you very much. I guess I really needed to hear that." She took a tissue from the box he held out to her and wiped her face.

"The perp is out there," the cop said. "Human beings do not disappear into thin air, no matter what the movies might want you to believe, with all the special effects they come up with."

"Joe's right. One hundred percent." Rick took her hand, and she held on hard. "Maybe Ash and Sandy will come up with a composite drawing," he said, "a drawing that will be faxed everywhere. And I mean throughout the entire country."

The idea reassured her and, inch by inch, Kristin could feel herself loosen up—first her neck, then her spine, then her fingers and toes. She breathed deeply, once, twice. Rick rose and stepped behind her, offering a massage that could have put her to sleep.

She heard him say something to Joe about the stress she'd been under.

"Magic hands," she murmured a minute later, her lids drooping.

He aborted his conversation with Joe Silva and breathed in her ear, "I'll take your word on that."

The nuance registered and so did the heat flowing through her body. And in a police station!

The telephone rang, startling Kristin.

Joe hung up quickly and said, "Sandy's got something. We can go in."

Ash and Sandy sat next to each other at an ordinary table. The sketch lay between them. It was upside down from where Kristin stood, but she could see a lot of work had been done.

"Hi, Mom." Her daughter's voice sounded thready, and Kristin quickly crossed the room, leaned down and hugged her.

"Wow! Look at all you've done today."

Besides the tattoo, she saw a round face with plump cheeks, deep-set brown eyes and an upturned, flat nose with nostrils showing. A blue ski cap covered the head and ears. Peeping out from one ear was a gold earring.

"She did fabulous work today," declared Sandy. "Ash, may I tell them how you described the jerk?"

Ashley nodded and buried her head in Kristin's shoulder.

"She remembered the brown eyes, but we also needed to get the shape of the head—round, narrow, long, square and so on. So when I asked about that, she said, 'Piggy. He looked like a pink pig.' Ergo, the nose."

Studying the picture, Rick said, "It could have been

broken and fixed badly—a lousy nose job. The end is made of cartilage and not too difficult to shape."

"I saw him in the hallway real fast," said Ashley, "right before…before…he grabbed me." She kept holding her mother, but spoke to Rick. "Did you tell them he was taller than you?"

"Do you still think so, sweetheart?"

The girl stood. So did he. She walked toward his right side and tilted her head. "Yes. Maybe only just as tall, but bigger." She motioned for him to lean down. "Come closer. I want to ask you something."

He squatted next to her and listened. Kristin watched every move.

"Can we leave now?" she whispered, but not so quietly that Kristin couldn't hear. "I want to go home to the lake."

"Sure, kiddo." He straightened to his six feet and signaled Kristin. "She's ready to leave."

"Are we done?" asked Kristin, glancing from Sandy to Joe.

"Let's ask Ashley," suggested Sandy, holding up the picture. "What do you think, Ash? Are we done?"

The child thought for a moment. "Well, he wore a coat—but that's not part of his face."

But Sandy immediately started sketching the shoulders. "Ski jacket? Or raincoat type?"

"Long."

"Like this?" asked the artist.

Ash nodded. "Now, we're done. Except…" She turned to Rick. "Remember what I said about his voice? Rough, like maybe salt and broken sea shells were in his throat."

Rick nodded. "You've said he sounded as if he had a bad cold. Maybe laryngitis?"

"I'm adding it to the description," said Sandy, writing quickly.

Joe Silva motioned to someone at the doorway and then started to clap his hands. Other officers entered and joined in the applause.

"Look at the great job Ashley's been able to do for us," said Joe, holding up the drawing. Words of praise came from every cop in the room. "One of you guys, get this wired out."

"And then he'll never be able to hurt anybody ever, ever again," Ashley said.

"That's right," said Kristin before she waved the cops closer. "Come meet my daughter, everybody. Put a face on who you're fighting for."

CHAPTER THIRTEEN

RICK'S PRIDE IN KRISTIN almost surpassed his love. Or maybe they were both part of the same emotion. He didn't analyze his feelings; he simply enjoyed them and kept them to himself. Especially when the *L* word sort of crept up on him. But once he began to recognize it, his feelings for Kristin only grew deeper. "Put a face on who you're fighting for," she'd said. She'd taken charge in that building. She and Ashley deserved a lot more than a spooked cop with little to offer.

"It's eleven o'clock," he said as they left the precinct. "We have a big decision." He opened the doors of the Pilot and watched Quincy spring into the backseat. "Lunch or ice cream?"

"Ice cream," Ashley responded immediately, climbing in after Quincy. "Ice cream, please. Can we go to Ripples? That's my favorite place. And we have treats for Quincy because he can't eat people sweets."

"Whatever she wants," said Kristin. "Today's her day." She glanced up at him, her blue eyes warm. "It's your day, too, Rick. Thank you so much for…for…" She gestured in a wide circle. "For everything."

"My pleasure," he murmured.

He leaned forward and kissed her. In front of the kid,

the dog, the pedestrians and cops. He couldn't help himself. He loved her.

But when he lifted his head and saw her surprise, he wanted to kick himself. Damn it. It wasn't the time or the place for a kiss. She'd simply been thanking him. And he'd overreacted because of that look in her eyes. It *could* have been love…. Now he wasn't sure, and suddenly felt the same way Ashley did. Morningstar Lake seemed like a wonderful destination—the sooner, the better.

"Lots of traffic today," he said, reaching for a safe topic as he pulled into his lane.

"It's always pretty awful around here on Saturdays," said Kristin. "But if we cut through one of the residential neighborhoods…coming up, see? Bainbridge Road. Make a right there, and we'll avoid a lot of cars and still get back onto the main road leading to Ripples."

He followed her directions for three streets, until they were blocked by a police car. The cops were running yellow tape, cordoning off the area. People were starting to gather in small groups.

"What the…?" said Rick, pulling to the curb and getting out of the car. He turned to the women. "I'll be right back."

Kristin nodded.

"Are you going to help someone?" asked Ashley.

"Just checking."

"His sister says he has to save the world," Kristin said to Ashley. "And I wish…it didn't have to be saved."

Rick walked away, not liking the sound of that. Not liking it at all.

Five minutes later, he had the information he needed, and jogged to the car.

"I'm going to be here awhile." He leaned in closer to Kristin, so Ash couldn't hear the details, and spoke quickly. "A domestic dispute. The woman secretly called 911 from another part of the house. The husband's carrying a handgun. Domestic violence is the worst kind. Hopefully, this might take some time but turn out well."

"Oh, my God," said Kristin. "A gun. The poor woman."

"The locals are waiting for a crisis team to arrive."

She gave him a half smile. "I'd guess the crisis team *has* arrived. At least part of it."

Maybe. "I'll see if I can help out. You take the car and get ice cream. Get lunch. Go back to your parents' home. Whatever. I'll call you later." He stroked her cheek, tapped the car and left without waiting for her answer.

KRISTIN WATCHED HIM join his brothers in blue. Of course he would jump in, put himself out there. It's what he did, who he was. He just didn't want to admit it. He liked saving the world....

Like he'd saved her? And Ashley? Were they just part and parcel of his personal modus operandi? Or was the light in his eye when he looked at her genuine? Was the thoughtful behavior he demonstrated every day—the good humor, the concern, his dependability—part of his deeper feelings for them? With this man, she'd learned that actions screamed much more loudly than words. But...she wanted the words, too. If they were true.

Being a cop had ruined his first marriage. The job was always the "other woman." Today, that concept was more than a theory. It was coming to life in front of her. And yet the whole situation seemed ludicrous on such a fine sunny day in June, under a clear blue sky.

She scanned the scene in front of her. The crowd had grown. She spotted Rick with a phone at his ear, and suddenly, nothing seemed ludicrous. Her stomach churned as reality hit with a vengeance. The hostage taker had a gun! A real gun. Her heart thudded; she tasted metal. Fear. Fear claimed her, every nerve, every pore, every part of her being.

What if the guy started shooting? What if he shot Rick? What if he shot the hostage? What if Rick wound up with nightmares again?

Kristin didn't want to leave, but she opened her door to switch seats. Ash deserved her ice cream.

"Mommy, what's going on?"

"I'm just getting behind the wheel. Rick needs to stay here to help."

"Then we can't go," her daughter said. "He might need us. Or Quincy. We're his *backup*. I learned that word."

Kris tried to lighten her voice. "Oh, he's got lots of buddies to help him out."

But Ashley shook her head, her mouth a hard line. "We have to stay, Mom. Please. We'll stay right here in the car. We won't go over there." She pointed in the direction of the developing incident, and then, with a crafty expression, added, "I'll have a huge dinner later. Okay?"

Kristin rummaged through her handbag. "How about a stick of gum for now?"

RICK MADE A QUICK CALL to Captain Stein to let him know he was on the job again. Of course, Stein had to say a few words about jumping into the deep end, after Rick explained the situation.

"It can't be helped, Captain. It seems I'm the primary, working out of a precinct vehicle. No one else is here yet except the street boys, but I think they'll be okay."

"I wasn't expecting the surprise, but you, Detective Cooper, are exactly where you're supposed to be. Keep in touch. And good luck."

Rick was used to being dispatched anywhere he was needed in the metropolitan area when crisis intervention teams were called. He never knew exactly what he'd find. Sometimes, an unlucky private citizen who happened to be on the scene before the special team arrived began the negotiations—an experience the individual would remember forever. Most times, however, the pros showed up quickly enough to take over.

Rick got out of the police car and surveyed his surroundings—the house, the yard, the front door, the side yards—glad the local officers had taped the full area and were pushing the crowd back. A quick glimpse over his shoulder showed him that Kristin and Ash were still parked. He wanted to jog over and send them on their way, but that was impossible now.

"Do we have the phone number for the house?" he asked one of the patrolmen.

"Affirmative. A technical equipment team is on the way."

"Good. I might need a uniform and a vest." The van would hold a lot of miscellaneous supplies.

Rick continued speaking. "You're my secondary for now. Take notes, keep me updated on new info as you gather it." He clapped the surprised young man on the shoulder—he looked almost as young as Danny to him. "You'll do fine. Let's call the house."

And in an instant, Rick had taken charge. As he'd done dozens of times in the past. It felt right. It felt comfortable.

The phone rang twice before the home owner picked up. Rick didn't have a chance to say hello.

"I see you out there. Now get out of my yard."

"That's just what we want to talk about. I'm Rick. And you're—" he checked his notes "—George. George Duncan. Do I have that right?"

There was no response.

"Can you give me an answer so the two of us can figure this all out?"

"Sure I can. And here's my answer. I got a gun, just like you. And guess what, Copper, it's loaded."

"I'm not using my gun, George. Not at all. I'm not even holding it. How about you?"

"My wife—she hates the gun."

George hadn't answered the question. *Assume he's holding the gun.* "Yeah. Most women hate them. So, what's been happening in your life, George?"

"What do you care?"

"I want to help you work it out." *And keep him talking.*

"No, you don't. You just want me out there so you can arrest me."

"I want to help you, George. Sometimes life's tough, isn't it?"

"Tough? Life sucks, ya know?"

"Sure I know. Sometimes it sucks big-time, with big problems."

"Yeah."

"Is that what's happening, George?"

"Yeah—big problems."

"Sometimes money can be a problem. But we can figure that out. Is it money, George?"

"A real man doesn't have money problems. My wife…"

He fell silent. *Not good.*

"How's your wife doing, George?"

"Better'n me. She's got a good job. Pays the friggin' mortgage. Do I need to see that every friggin' month?"

"Oh, that could be tough. So what kind of work do you do, George?"

Rick eyeballed the area. It seemed the full crisis team had arrived. The young cop was going between him and the technical equipment van, and the perimeter guys were feeding him more information about the family inside.

Good. Rick could concentrate on his own part, his goals—to build a rapport with George, get him to surrender peacefully and get the wife out safely. If only the man didn't have that gun. Time was Rick's best ally, and he would take all the time in the world to make this go down right.

George threatened to use his weapon. Threats to the cops, threats to his wife. But he hadn't used it. So something was stopping him. The money problems led to job problems, depression, fear, marital problems—all the gremlins came out little by little, as Rick asked probing questions and commiserated with him. The two-hour mark felt like ten.

"We can help you get a job," Rick said. "That's for sure. No problem there. We've got a whole committee of experts who specialize in jobs." He could promise that because it was true. There were scores of social services in the area. "How does that sound?"

"A good job. With real money."

They'd made significant progress and were bargaining now. They were heading to the termination phase, which was usually brief but could sometimes be violent.

"You'll have job choices," Rick said. "You pick."

"Okay."

Bingo. "So, George, this is what we do now." He checked out the rest of the team. SWAT was there with their sharpshooters, his secondary was taking notes. Rick covered his phone and spoke softly to the younger cop. "Tell SWAT he might be coming out now, hopefully with no gun."

He caught sight of a video camera. Geez. The media was there, too. When did that happen? He refocused on the hostage taker.

"George, this is Rick again. All you need to do now is leave your gun in the house, come to the front door and walk outside." He spoke slowly, carefully. "Just hold your hands up to show they're empty. You're going to be okay."

He waited. They all waited. The door opened. The threshold remained empty for ten seconds. A very long ten seconds. Then George came out, hands up, and surrendered. It was over. Some officers went inside to find the wife and retrieve the gun.

Rick leaned against the car, physically weak with relief.

"Good job, Detective Cooper. We're lucky you happened to be around." The incident commander who had orchestrated the entire encounter after Rick's arrival extended his hand.

"Thanks. You have a good crew here."

"Thank you. We need you to debrief with everyone else. Don't leave."

Rick nodded. "Understood." He scanned the vicinity and spotted his car. "I'll be right back."

Kristin met him halfway. With arms wide, and a kiss as sweet as victory. He held on to her and felt her tremble. His doubts returned full blast.

"Krissy, Krissy." So sweet, so giving. He didn't want to leave her. But the truth had to be faced.

She beat him to it. "Congratulations on your new job! I guess you found what you'd been missing."

"Crazy, isn't it? Lost and found right where I began." It seemed like some conspiracy, and a trite one at that. He shrugged.

"So, you'll forget about security jobs, law school, music…"

"I know you're thinking that this is no way to live," he began. "You're shaking, you're scared. And this—" he gestured to the cordoned-off area "—is a typical situation. We get DV calls, uh, that's domestic violence, all the time."

"I know," she whispered.

"This is my work," he said apologetically. "I don't know why, but it's what I seem to do."

She began to chuckle, and placed her palms on his cheeks. "I know why. You're making a difference in this world. You just saved a life, Rick! In fact, two lives. And that is not a small thing."

His thoughts raced. She was right. His sister was right. Being a warrior for the underdog was who he'd always been. Despite failure. Despite pain and major self-doubt. Somehow, he always managed to climb back on the stubborn horse.

But it was no life for a married man or a family. And

certainly not for Kristin, who still seemed shaken by this incident.

"I've gotta get back," he said quickly. But then he saw Ash and the shepherd coming toward him.

"Hey, kiddo. How're you doing?"

She stared up at him with those big blue eyes. *Uh-oh.* He was back to being Santa Claus.

"Rick—you saved him and the lady. But I was so scared for her, and you, and your friends. For everybody."

"We're trained to handle this kind of situation, Ash."

"Well, good job!" She gave him a high five, then pointed at the victim, the wife, who was surrounded by family and police. And who was crying.

"I think Quincy and I should visit her. She must be scared."

He looked at Kristin, who, with mouth agape, simply stared at her daughter. He didn't blame her.

"That's one heck of a child you're raising, Kris. I know she's going to be just fine. In fact, she's almost there right now."

Even if they never caught the perp who'd hurt her, Ash was healing. She wanted to help others, and that would change a horrible experience into something positive. She'd also become a lot more self-confident.

He leaned down. "The lady has lots of friends with her, Ash, but I'm awfully proud of you. You'll always be my special kiddo."

She started to smile, then cocked her head. "You're in a minor key again. You sound…sad."

"I'm fine, honey, but the team is waiting for me." He pointed back to the officers involved, then spoke to Kristin again. "Take the car. I'll get a ride to Ripples and meet you when I'm done. You must be starving by now."

"All right," she said slowly, studying him. "We'll see you there." She motioned to Ashley, and they headed back to the car.

He watched them go, shaking his head at Ashley's ever-sharp ears, and returned to the scene.

ASHLEY WASN'T the only person in her family with good ears. If ever Kristin had heard "goodbye," today was the day. Now that Rick was back in work mode, his personal demons had come back to haunt him. Relationships, commitments, a "private" life away from the force. His divorce.

She blinked quickly, overruling the disappointment that threatened to submerge her. So what if his marriage hadn't succeeded? Did that mean he could never love again? Never try again?

She started the car while a kaleidoscope of their life at the lake rotated through her mind. Rick and Ashley making music on the porch, Rick and Quincy jogging together, Rick coming from the lake a total mess, Rick directing traffic, Rick and she in each other's arms.

He had a heart as big as New York itself, and she loved the man he was, cop or no cop. She certainly hadn't been searching for love when she and Ash had gone to Morningstar Lake. She had actually never thought much about it since John had died. But with Rick, the joy had come back, and amazingly, love had bloomed again.

And Rick? She knew his feelings matched hers. He just didn't say the words. But she'd seen the love in his eyes when he didn't realize it showed. He'd dropped his guard the night they'd returned from the club, and when he'd looked at Ash and Quincy and her as a family.

As for today—so what if his doubts about them had resurfaced after he was back in action a little while ago? She had doubts, too—his job was dangerous. But she didn't want to give up the love of a wonderful person because of fear. She was trying to teach Ashley not to give in to fear. She had to set an example. And loving Rick was the best example of all.

She could erase his doubts. She'd find the right words. Damn it. She wasn't going to stand by idly and let him throw away a wonderful future together.

Kristin drove, tapping the steering wheel, trying to figure out how to convince him of that wonderful future she envisioned. She stopped at the last corner on the edge of the neighborhood where Rick was debriefing. She made a right turn onto the main road and glanced at her daughter in the front passenger seat. Ash was fiddling with the radio.

Kristin started to laugh.

"What, Mom?"

"Any other mother would know exactly what to expect when their kid got her hands on the radio. But you? I never know. Will it be Tchaikovsky, Stan Getz or rock and roll?"

Ashley giggled. "I like everything. But you know what, Mom?"

"What?"

"I think it's time to choose," she replied.

Great timing. A good conversation was exactly what they needed right now. Something to distract Ash when they drove past the mall and theater in just a couple of minutes. If this traffic would let up, she'd whiz by in a blur. She hoped she wouldn't get stuck at a light up there.

"Why choose? Daddy said you never needed to. Just have fun with your music."

Her daughter's head was moving up and down. "That's just it, Mom. I've been thinking about it ever since I yelled at Madison to get serious. Remember all the questions I had for Mrs. Shilling? Remember how I've practiced? It's fun. I like practicing. I like getting better and better, and I want to be good—really, really good."

"Carnegie Hall good?" asked Kristin, while dollar signs floated through her mind. The Juilliard School or the Boston Conservatory. A lot more expensive than a state college. She had to get her own career back on track. "So tell me more, Ash."

"It's like you and math," her daughter replied. "You like complicated problems. The harder, the better. That's how I feel. Daddy once said that if I didn't know what I wanted to do, I should stick to the classics. So I will do that— because I just like them. Do you think I should ask Rick?"

"Oh, honey. Rick's a jazz man. No secret there."

"But I think he... Mom! Look! Look!"

Caught. The mall was on the right side, the entrance to the movies a mere half block away. She'd almost made it. "You're in the car with me, Ash. It's okay. We'll be gone from here in a moment."

But her daughter was leaning forward, straining the seat belt and staring out the window. Pointing. "That's him! The man who hurt me. I know it. It's him."

Kristin's blood turned icy. "Are you sure, Ash?" If so, then the guy must live in the area.

"Yes, yes. We gotta do something!"

She couldn't see clearly, but she believed her daughter. Where to park, where to park…

"*Harry Potter*'s playing and a new *Shrek*. Mommy, there's lots and lots of kids going in there." Ash's shrill voice told its own story. Quincy leaned over from the backseat and started licking Ashley, already reacting to her distress.

Kris pulled the car into a bus stop and jumped out. "Call Rick on the cell phone, Ashley. Now! Stay in the car and lock the doors. Got it?"

HE WAS STILL ELBOW DEEP in forms and the personnel debriefing when his phone rang. *Kris*. Maybe plans had changed. Maybe the ice cream place had closed down. He looked at his team. "Hang on a sec." Then spoke into the phone. "Cooper."

He couldn't understand a word. Ashley. That's all he knew. Ashley screaming. Ashley hysterical.

His heart raced, but his words were calm and clear. "Slowly, Ash. Talk slowly." He heard her take a huge breath. He listened in disbelief. "Your mother…what?" he almost shouted. So much for keeping his cool. "Sit tight. I'm on my way." He jerked toward the others. "I need a driver. Now!"

"I'm with you." It was his young secondary, who pointed at his car.

"Let's go." Rick started jogging. "Code three with lights and sirens. But we may need more." He turned around. "The perp that raped Ashley McCarthy on your turf three months ago is back. At that mall. Joe Silva's in charge. You can call him to check me out. I may need backup."

Instantly, another squad car filled up and followed his lead, sirens blaring, lights flashing. The results were magical. Civilian cars disappeared and the road opened up. Beautiful.

He turned to the driver. "Step on it."

IN HER RUNNING SHOES, Kristin approached her target from behind. She reached high to tap his shoulder.

"Hey, mister. You got the time?"

He half turned around, purple tattoo on his plump cheek. "What?"

"That's him, Mom," Ashley screamed. With the car window down, her voice was clear. "That's him!"

His startled expression was shaded by a split second of recognition as he stared at Ashley. It was the confirmation Kristin needed, but the guy didn't wait. He took off down the block, Kristin in pursuit.

Adrenaline gave her feet wings. She flew after him with Olympic speed. Pedestrians on the sidewalk began to take notice, moving out of the way.

"Stop him!" Kris shouted, just before she sprang onto his back like a jungle cat onto its larger prey. She punched his ears, grabbed him around the throat and pressed as hard as she could.

"For my daughter, you stinking piece of filth." *Soft spots, soft spots. Get his soft spots.* She wanted the eyes, but she had no more fingers.

He kept running, but he pulled at her arms at the same time, as if she were nothing more than a mere annoyance. Her hold loosened and she felt herself slip. She landed hard on the sidewalk, her breath gone, but frustration giving her strength. He'd continued to run. She staggered to her feet, ready to try again—and felt a breeze touch her skin. A breeze from a silver blur.

With a feral growl, a hundred pounds of pure canine muscle whizzed by. In a nanosecond, Quincy leaped from the ground to the perp's back and took him down. The man lay on the sidewalk, on his stomach, not moving. Just swearing, sweating and praying.

A circle formed around them, people steering clear of what seemed to be a very healthy gray wolf. Kristin trotted right over.

"Good job, Quince." She petted him. "Oh, you're such a good boy."

Of course, the dog wanted to kiss her and play again. To him it was a game. She pointed at the suspect. "Stay, Quincy."

The dog resumed guarding the prone perp. She stared at the man who'd caused so much pain. "Mister, you make one move and you're dead. I don't care about your rights. I don't care about your health. Just like you didn't care about my daughter's."

"You're crazy, lady. Friggin' crazy." He had a low and gravelly voice.

"Crazy like a mother."

People were talking, asking questions, using their cell phones. Sirens wailed in the distance. *Thank God.*

Kristin kept her eye on the perp and addressed the crowd at the same time. "I live in this town, just like most of you. He nabbed my daughter in this very movie theater three months ago and hurt her—badly."

When a rumble ran through the group, she knew they understood. Where was Rick? Was Ash still in the car?

The sirens blared loudly now, and from the corner

of her eye she saw red and blue lights. They seemed fuzzy. Someone was using a bullhorn. The noise hammered at her head. Nausea threatened. But through it she was able to focus on her daughter's high-pitched voice. Ash had left the car. At least she'd waited for the action to be over.

"Rick! Rick! Quincy got him, Mommy got him. Come here."

And then he was in front of her. "Kristin…"

"Thanks." She felt herself go limp. "I can't…"

HE CAUGHT HER before she hit the ground, but gave orders at the same time. "Cuff the suspect, search him, Mirandize him and take him in. Call an ambulance. Ashley, stay with me." He motioned to Quincy to guard her.

Rick gazed at the woman in his arms, his stomach tight. He wanted to kiss her and kill her at the same time. What had she been thinking, to go after the guy by herself?

Someone produced a blanket and he began to lay her down. She stirred. Her eyelids flickered.

"Did you get him?"

"*You* got him. You and Quincy. I was part of the cleanup crew." He spoke softly, although he wanted to scream at her. "We've got an ambulance coming. We're going to check you out."

Wrong thing to say. She started to sit up. "I'm fine. I'm fine. I think I was just scared."

Of course she'd been scared. What did she expect?

"Where's Ash?" she asked, scanning the area.

"Right here," said the child, her arm around the dog. "You know what, Mom? You're a hero! You jumped on him like Spiderman, except you'd be Spiderwoman."

Rick winced. The outcome could have been so different. "The EMTs are here, Krissy, and you're going to let them examine you."

She began to protest, then glimpsed his thunderous expression and shut up.

He nodded. "Good girl."

His secondary came up to him. "We've interviewed a bunch of people here. Their statements are variations of the same story." He peered at the dog and shook his head. "And I hate to tell you how many pictures they took with their cell phone cameras when it was going down. It'll be all over the Internet."

"Just what we don't need."

"And on the local news." His buddy nodded toward the sidewalk, where a television crew was filming and reporting.

"Damn it," Rick muttered. "Maybe folks will watch a baseball game instead."

The other man shook his head. "I don't know if a World Series game could compete with this event."

Just then, a news reporter approached. "Can we get the story behind the story? We know what people saw. What's the reason?"

Rick replied. "Citizens and police worked together and a man was brought to justice. That's the story." He walked away as his imagination started working overtime. It could have ended differently. Very badly. Kristin…Ashley… He started to shake. The perp could have been armed. He spun around.

"Was he searched?"

"Affirmative. Armed and dangerous. One mother of a knife."

FIFTEEN MINUTES LATER, Kristin sat next to Rick in the front seat of his vehicle, with Ash and Quincy in the back. Everyone together again.

"We have to press charges, but that can wait until tomorrow morning," Rick said, turning on the ignition. "Still want Ripples?"

"No," Ashley piped up. "Let's go home. We can give Quincy water and food…oh, we have no food, do we, Mom? Not for dogs or people."

Kristin turned around to study her daughter. "Home? Are you sure, Ash?"

"Yes. You got him, Mom. He's in jail, so I'm not so afraid anymore. I'm sure glad we went to self-defense classes. So let's go home. Maybe Grandma and Grandpa will come over."

Home sounded wonderful to Kristin, too. She looked at Rick. "Is that okay with you?"

"Anything you want." He stared straight ahead, and her heart hit the ground. She was losing him. She took a deep breath.

"What I want…is you," she said quietly. "I love you, Rick."

In a second, his seat belt was off and he was kissing her as though she was going to disappear in a moment. She wrapped her arms around his neck, glad the transmission was on the steering column and not the floor.

"I love you, too. I adore you, and you almost killed me back there. You can never, never do that again. No more heroics. Call the cops, for God's sake. Ash was smarter than you. She used the phone."

"Okay. No more heroics."

Suspicion was written all over his face. "That's it? No argument?"

"No argument."

"I don't trust you," he said slowly. "You're too easy."

"I'm in the insurance business. Another adventure for an amateur carries too much risk."

He kissed her again.

Delicious. "Uh—Rick? Could you just say those three little words again?"

A ruddy face didn't stop him. "I love you. Very, very much… Are six words okay?"

"Oh, yeah…"

She watched the expression on his face change from delight to concern. He had more to say.

"What about my job? It's really my career," he said slowly. "Do you hate it?"

She cupped his cheek. "I'm frightened. Why wouldn't I be? But I also figured out something else from watching you, and Sam, and the police force right here."

"You did? We're just doing what we're paid to do."

"But you're doing it so well—and that's the point. If people like you aren't around to protect the rest of us, then everyone's daughter is at risk."

He kissed her again. "So smart."

"And so yucky, yucky, yucky," said a giggling voice from the backseat.

An hour later, after stopping at the supermarket for basics and picking up Chinese takeout, they were in Kristin's driveway. The lawn service had done its job; nothing was overgrown. Light shone from inside due to the electric timers she'd set. The brick ranch-style house appeared lived in and unremarkable.

But Kristin was watching Ashley and waiting for her reaction. She needn't have been concerned. Ash jumped out of the car, took a grocery bag and marched up the driveway to the back of the house, to their usual entrance through the kitchen.

Kristin beamed. "My old Ashley is coming back. Life will be easier now."

"Easier with a soon-to-be teenager?" Rick teased, reaching for a bag of food.

Her cell rang before she could respond to him. They continued toward the door as she answered it. "Marsha! Hi. On the news? Really? Yes, we're fine. All of us." She spoke a moment longer and hung up.

They entered the house to see Ash already setting the table for their meal, while Quincy drank water from a plastic bowl. Ashley pointed to the dog. "It was the biggest thing I could find. He's such a slurper."

The house phone rang. Kristin picked up the receiver. "Jo Anne! Yes, we're here. Ashley's fine. Just a minute and I'll ask her."

This was the big one. The big question. "Ash, Sabrina wants to talk to you." She held out the phone, and her daughter took it from her.

"Hi, Sabrina." A smile grew on Ashley's face as she listened. She tapped Kristin's arm. "Mom, can Sabrina come over?"

Did a day have twenty-four hours? "Yes. Of course. Anytime."

"She wants to bring Mary Beth and their instruments. They've been waiting for me."

"Sure, sweetheart. Bring the whole orchestra. We're back!" Finally, they sat down to eat, and Rick's cell phone rang.

"Cooper." Kristin watched his face light up. He stared at Ashley. "For you."

She gestured to herself. *Me?* "Hello? Madison! Yeah. That was us. And your uncle, too. Where are you? Hang on." She looked at Kristin. "Mom, can Madison come over, too? With her mom and dad and Danny? In an hour."

Kristin nodded, her mind racing. Coffee, cake. She had nothing in the house. She mouthed her request to Rick.

He took the phone. "The answer's yes, but where's your mother?" He only waited a moment. "Pile in the car, bring Mom and Dad, and a lot of desserts. The cupboard's pretty barren here."

An everyday atmosphere returned to the kitchen. Their meal disappeared quickly. Ashley patted her stomach and glanced around the table. "We're such a great team," she said with a sigh. "Just like a regular family."

The silence became intense. Kristin gazed at the back wall.

"Kristin?" Rick's soft voice made her name sound like a prayer. "A family?"

She turned toward him, saw the love he had for her so clearly written on his face, and smiled. "If you're asking, the answer is a definite yes," she said. "A regular family."

Then she was in his arms, receiving and giving kisses, hugs and promises. And commitments.

"I love you, Kristin. So much. For so long…"

"It's mutual, Rick. I love you, too." She snuggled closer. "I could stay here forever."

"A very good idea," he said, his voice trembling, "because I'll be holding you forever." He kissed her again.

A soft click sounded. With a big grin on her face, Ashley held up Rick's cell phone. A snapshot. "Busted," she said. "And you're picture perfect. Get it? I made a word joke."

Kristin poked Rick, and they laughed along with the child they would raise together in the future. Then Quincy trotted to Ashley, nuzzled her and barked his approval, definitely having the last word.

* * * * *

*In honor of our 60th anniversary,
Harlequin® American Romance® is celebrating by
featuring an all-American male each month, all
year long with*
MEN MADE IN AMERICA!
*This June, we'll be featuring American men living
in the West.*

Here's a sneak preview of
THE CHIEF RANGER by Rebecca Winters.

*Chief Ranger Vance Rossiter has to confront the sister
of a man who died while under Vance's watch...and
also confront his attraction to her.*

"Chief Ranger Rossiter?" The sight of the woman who'd stepped inside Vance's office brought him to his feet. "I'm Rachel Darrow. Your secretary said I should come right in."

"Please," he said, walking around his desk to shake her hand. At a glance he estimated she was in her mid-twenties. Her feminine curves did wonders for the pale blue T-shirt and jeans she was wearing. "Ranger Jarvis informed me there's a young boy with you."

The unfriendly expression in her beautiful green eyes caught him off guard. "Yes," was her clipped reply. "When we arrived in Yosemite the ranger told me I couldn't go anywhere in the park until I talked to you first."

"That's right."

"Knowing you wanted this meeting to be private, he offered to show my nephew around Headquarters."

So this woman was the victim's sister…. "What's his name?"

"Nicky."

The boy who haunted Vance's dreams now had a name. "How old is he?"

"He turned six three weeks ago. Were you the man in charge when my brother and sister-in-law were killed?"

"Yes. To tell you I'm sorry for what happened couldn't begin to convey my feelings."

The woman's gaze didn't flicker. "I won't even try to describe mine. Just tell me one thing. Was their accident preventable?"

"Yes," he answered without hesitation.

"In other words, the people working under you fell asleep on your watch and two lives were snuffed out as a result."

Hearing it put like that, he had to set the record straight. "My staff had nothing to do with it. I, myself, could have prevented the loss of life."

Ms. Darrow's expression hardened. "So you admit culpability."

"Yes. I take full blame."

A look of pain crossed over her features. "You can just stand there and admit it?" Her cry echoed that of his own tortured soul.

"Yes." He sucked in his breath.

"I work for a cruise line. Aboard ship, it's the captain's responsibility to maintain rigid safety regulations. If a disaster like that had happened while he was in charge he would have been relieved of his command and never given another ship again."

Rachel Darrow couldn't know she was preaching to the converted. "If you've come to the park with the intention of bringing a lawsuit against me for negligence, maybe you should." It would only be what he deserved.

"Maybe I will."

In the next instant, she wheeled around and hurried out of his office. Vance could have gone after her, but it would cause a scene, something he was loath to do for a variety of reasons. In the first place, he needed to cool down before he approached her again.

The discovery of the Darrows' frozen bodies had affected every ranger in the park. A little boy had been orphaned—a boy whose aunt was all he had left.

* * * * *

Will Rachel allow Vance to explain—and will she let
him into her heart?
Find out in
THE CHIEF RANGER
Available June 2009 from
Harlequin® American Romance®.

We'll be spotlighting a different series every month
throughout 2009 to celebrate our 60th anniversary.

Look for Harlequin®
American Romance® in June!

Join us for a year-long celebration of the rugged
American male! From cops to cowboys—
Men Made in America has the hero
you've been dreaming about!

Look for

The Chief Ranger
by Rebecca Winters, on sale in June!

HARLEQUIN® *Romance*®

Escape Around the World
Dream destinations, whirlwind weddings!

Honeymoon with the Boss
by
JESSICA HART

Top tycoon Tom Maddison is used to calling the shots—until his convenient marriage falls through. But rather than waste his honeymoon, he'll take his boardroom to the beach and bring his oh-so-sensible secretary Imogen on a tropical business trip! But will Tom finally see the sexy woman that prudent Imogen truly is?

Available in June wherever books are sold.

REQUEST YOUR FREE BOOKS!

2 FREE NOVELS PLUS 2 FREE GIFTS!

HARLEQUIN®

Super Romance®

Exciting, emotional, unexpected!

YES! Please send me 2 FREE Harlequin® Superromance® novels and my 2 FREE gifts (gifts are worth about $10). After receiving them, if I don't wish to receive any more books, I can return the shipping statement marked "cancel." If I don't cancel, I will receive 6 brand-new novels every month and be billed just $4.69 per book in the U.S. or $5.24 per book in Canada. That's a savings of close to 15% off the cover price! It's quite a bargain! Shipping and handling is just 50¢ per book*. I understand that accepting the 2 free books and gifts places me under no obligation to buy anything. I can always return a shipment and cancel at any time. Even if I never buy another book from Harlequin, the two free books and gifts are mine to keep forever.

135 HDN EYLG   336 HDN EYLS

Name	(PLEASE PRINT)

Address	Apt. #

City	State/Prov.	Zip/Postal Code

Signature (if under 18, a parent or guardian must sign)

Mail to the **Harlequin Reader Service:**
IN U.S.A.: P.O. Box 1867, Buffalo, NY 14240-1867
IN CANADA: P.O. Box 609, Fort Erie, Ontario L2A 5X3

Not valid to current subscribers of Harlequin Superromance books.

**Are you a current subscriber of Harlequin Superromance books
and want to receive the larger-print edition?
Call 1-800-873-8635 today!**

* Terms and prices subject to change without notice. Prices do not include applicable taxes. Sales tax applicable in N.Y. Canadian residents will be charged applicable provincial taxes and GST. Offer not valid in Quebec. This offer is limited to one order per household. All orders subject to approval. Credit or debit balances in a customer's account(s) may be offset by any other outstanding balance owed by or to the customer. Please allow 4 to 6 weeks for delivery. Offer available while quantities last.

Your Privacy: Harlequin is committed to protecting your privacy. Our Privacy Policy is available online at www.eHarlequin.com or upon request from the Reader Service. From time to time we make our lists of customers available to reputable third parties who may have a product or service of interest to you. If you would prefer we not share your name and address, please check here. ☐

HSR09R

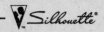

SPECIAL EDITION

FROM *USA TODAY* BESTSELLING AUTHOR
MARIE FERRARELLA

THE ALASKANS

LOVING THE RIGHT BROTHER

When tragedy struck, Irena Yovich headed
back to Alaska to console her ex-boyfriend's
family. While there she began seeing his brother,
Brody Hayes, in a very different light. Things
were about to really heat up. Had she fallen
for the wrong brother?

*Available in June
wherever books are sold.*

COMING NEXT MONTH

Available June 9, 2009

#1566 A SMALL-TOWN HOMECOMING • Terry McLaughlin
Built to Last
The return of architect Tess Roussel to her hometown has put her on a collision course with John Jameson Quinn. The contractor has her reeling...his scandalous past overshadows everything. Tess wants to believe that the contractor is deserving of her professional admiration and her trust, but her love, too?

#1567 A HOLIDAY ROMANCE • Carrie Alexander
A summer holiday in the desert? What had Alice Potter been thinking? If it wasn't for resort manager Kyle Jarreau, her dream vacation would be a nightmare. But can they keep their fling a secret...? For Kyle's sake, they *have* to.

#1568 FROM FRIEND TO FATHER • Tracy Wolff
Reece Sandler never planned to raise his daughter with Sarah Martin. They were only friends when she agreed to be his surrogate. Now things have changed and they have to be parents—together. Fine. Easy. But only if Reece can control his attraction to Sarah.

#1569 BEST FOR THE BABY • Ann Evans
9 Months Later
Pregnant and alone, Alaina Tillman returns to Lake Harmony and Zack Davidson, her girlhood love. Yet as attracted as she is to him, life isn't just about the two of them anymore. She has to do what's best for her baby. Does that mean letting Zack in—or pushing him away?

#1570 NO ORDINARY COWBOY• Mary Sullivan
Home on the Ranch
A ranch is so not Amy Graves's scene. Still, she promised to help, so here she is. Funny thing is she starts to feel at home. And even funnier, she starts to fall for a cowboy—Hank Shelter. As she soon discovers, however, there's nothing ordinary about him.

#1571 ALL THAT LOVE IS • Ginger Chambers
Everlasting Love
Jillian Davis was prepared to walk away from her marriage. But when her husband, Brad, takes her on a shortcut, an accident nearly kills them. Now, with the SUV as their fragile shelter, Jillian's only hope lies with the man she was ready to leave behind forever....

HSRCNMBPA0509